Who Said That?

The prequel to Hebridean Storm

By Libby Patterson

Published by Libby Patterson

Copyright © 2017 Libby Patterson

Kindle Edition, License Notes

This ebook is licensed for your personal enjoyment only. This ebook may not be re-sold or given away to other people. If you would like to share this book with another person, please purchase an additional copy for each recipient. If you are reading this book and did not purchase it, or it was not purchased for your use only, then please return to Amazon.com and purchase your own copy. Thank you for respecting the hard work of this author.

This book is a work of fiction. Names, characters, places and incidents are the product of the author's imagination or are used fictitiously. Any resemblance to actual events, locales or persons, living or dead, is coincidental.

Who Said That? is a work of fiction, however, it is based on our real life family experiences. It is written to thank all those who supported us and to pay tribute to all those suffering from mental health problems, I dedicate this story to you.

Chapter One

Seonag Macaulay fell in love with her son from the moment she saw him. She had been an older mother. She hadn't quite given up hope of having children but had stopped expecting them. She was to be doubly blessed a couple of years later with twin girls, but she obviously didn't know that in the July of 1988. The bubbly baby boy with his sprout of ginger curls was the be all and end all of her world.

The baby boy grew into a happy child, with a cheeky sense of humour that was evident from his early years. He was an inquisitive child, who was into everything and who loved the great outdoors. Uist provided the ideal playground for this free spirit who was in his element camping on the beach or roaming in the hills. Keeping up with Matt kept everyone fit.

School was a challenge, not because he couldn't keep up, but he had a short attention span with little time for what he considered as pointless rules. He wanted to get on with things, and gained a reputation for devising audacious schemes when the teachers attempted to keep him in line. His friends knew that when Matt Macaulay muttered that he "had a plan," they were in for some fun.

He thrived in maths but only achieved most of his other Standard Grades because a jobs-worth teacher told him that he was going to fail and achieve nothing in life. He passed Higher in English by reading the "crammer books" rather than the actual novels he was meant to be studying.

Out of school it was a different matter. He joined the cadets at the age of eleven and hung on every word they said until the age of sixteen. It was a small, local unit that gave him the stimulation he needed to grow in self confidence and develop his natural abilities. He would come home covered from head to toe in mud and camo paint. There were times when his mum would make him get changed by the back door as there was no way she was having half the machair in her kitchen.

That he would join the services was somehow inevitable from an early age but many were surprised that it was the Royal Navy rather than the Army. Matt had done his homework and well knew the career path he wanted to take... he had a plan. When he was called up for interview his parents talked to him about the reality and consequences of his planned career...it wouldn't be like the cadets. He thought for a moment then explained. "We all see things on the TV or in the news and think how terrible, there are some really bad things going on in the world. Most people can't do anything about it, they are not in a position to, but the people who can, must, or at least try, or where would we be? I have to give it a go."

And that is what he did. He trained initially in disaster recovery, being part of an elite squad, sent around the world to rescue people from both man made and environmental situations. His ability to assess a situation and find novel solutions soon became noticed, so much so that his remit broadened into understanding and neutralising the threats before they could do any real damage, the man made ones anyway.

They gave him the title of "Training Officer." This allowed him to slip between units, in and out of countries unnoticed, both assessing and providing invaluable "training" in dealing with the opposition. To maintain his cover and to share his techniques he was invited back to the 42 Commando training base in Plymouth. It was here, ironically, that the problems started.

The first time he blacked out was in the officers' mess. It was his first night back. When the medics found nothing wrong, it was put down to exhaustion and a bit too much to drink. Matt was adamant that he was not drunk, but thought no more of it. When others who witnessed it ribbed him because they said he didn't so much fall, as fold himself neatly onto the floor. He laughed it off, agreeing that yes, he even knew how to fall down without hurting himself. It was all part of the plan.

Just over a week later it happened again. Matt had been invited to join a week sixteen training squad. The training sergeant had noticed one recruit who showed particular potential. Matt was asked for his view on him.

Matt gave a talk and then worked the group through some role play scenarios to explore tactics. He found this more nerve wracking than being in the field, but it didn't show. The recruits were engaged and seemed to enjoy the session. To build on the relationship Matt decided to join the group for their twelve mile run. It had been a while since he had done that sort of exercise, but he was looking forward to it.

It was a dry, but overcast day. Good running weather. Matt enjoyed the banter with the younger men at the start, as far as he was concerned there was no question that he would keep up and show a few how it was to be done along the way. His career didn't depend on completing the distance as theirs' did.

At the ten mile mark he was comfortably with the front runners. There were a couple of diehards who streaked on ahead and there had been a time when Matt would have felt the need to keep up with them but today he was happy in the pack. It was because he felt relaxed and not pushing himself that he was so cross with himself when he fainted just short of the eleven mile point. One moment he was pleased that he could see the mile marker ahead, the next he was flat on his back peering at a circle of faces looking down on him, asking if he was alright. No warning; he didn't hurt himself and felt right as rain again in a few minutes.

This time the medics gave him a more thorough going over, yet the blood tests and ECG all came back clear. Meeting up with the camp doctor the next day and having his blood pressure taken for the umpteenth time, Matt admitted that he hadn't taken any time off since his father had died suddenly. Throwing himself into his work had been his way of coping. The doctor suggested that he should take more time for himself. He only had two weeks left of the posting in Plymouth which would not be too demanding, then after that he should think about a holiday. Matt agreed because that is what you did to get out of meetings with the doc. There was nothing wrong with him really. At least nothing that he wanted to think about at any rate.

It was late Friday afternoon as Matt walked across the parade ground back to his accommodation block. He began to feel lethargic and weary. "Not surprising ," he thought, "all these quacks poking at you." He had a couple of hours before dinner. Maybe he would take the advice and have a couple of hours rest. Perhaps the run had taken it out of him after all.

Lying on his bed Matt dozed in and out of sleep. As was his habit, he slept with his bedroom window open. Every now and again he thought he could hear people talking. They were mumbling, he couldn't make out what they were saying. He woke up at one point and looked out of the window. There were a few people hanging around outside. Matt pulled the window shut with a thump. He was annoyed. They must have been talking loudly to sound so close.

Matt did not feel much better but decided that this lying around was not for him, it was just making him grumpy. He'd have a shower and go down to the bar. He didn't make it down to the bar that evening, nor did he tell anyone that he passed out in the shower.

Matt kept a low profile over the weekend, he watched films and ordered takeaways. He turned down several invitations to go out, blaming doctor's instructions. He didn't feel unwell as such, but he was very self conscious about the possibility of fainting again; especially in front of people. He hated the fuss. He needed his sisters or one of his friends from home to take the piss out of him. That would make him feel better, he joked to himself.

The following week Matt was lecturing again. He enjoyed the interaction with the recruits. He felt that the weekend's rest had done him good. He started the week sitting down as he gave his talks... He said it was to be more relaxed and less formal. By Thursday he was he was back in full military mode, firing on all cylinders. On the Friday it happened again.

The morning began with a planning and tactics session. Matt had given the recruits a real scenario and invited them to find solutions. The recruits responded well enjoying the lively discussion. The conversations continued on the way down the stairs to the canteen for a well earned coffee break. As Matt turned to respond to a point being made behind him it all went black. He awoke at the bottom of the stairs, but this time something was different. There were one or two people standing over him, but more were concerned with a commotion further along the corridor. "What's happening?" asked Matt as he tried to sit himself up and look around.

"It's Toby ,sir," said an anxious young face. "As you fell you knocked into him. He fell too, looks like he's broken his leg."

Matt sat and watched as the medics gave the young recruit gas and air as they strapped his leg and drove him to hospital. Someone was talking to him, he didn't respond, listening instead to the fading wail of the ambulance siren. He felt sick to the stomach.

"Macaulay," a sharp voice interrupted his thoughts. "Let's get you over to the medical centre."

A medical orderly insisted in supporting Matt by the arm and leading him back to the doctor's office. Matt was sure he could hear people muttering as they passed. He couldn't see who it was. He didn't blame them. He felt guilty as hell. He was expecting to be reprimanded. Part of him would have welcomed the punishment.

Matt was led into a little side room adjoining the doctor's office where there were two shabby leather armchairs and a completely empty wooden desk. He could hear the doctor talking, but he didn't know to whom. He slouched into one of the chairs.

Major Sims the camp doctor came in and sat down beside him in the other chair. "I've ordered us both tea. I thought you could do with some, I certainly do."
"Thanks," muttered Matt. He wasn't expecting pleasantries.

"I got word that the young lad is going to be fine. Now we just need to work out what to do with you."

Matt closed his eyes and breathed a sigh of relief. He tried to clear his head but he felt as if he was in a noisy pub and had to concentrate on what the doctor was saying.

"What do you mean?"

" Well firstly, after we have had our tea I will need you to give me a urine sample."

" What?" Matt was suddenly very focussed.

" I've tested for everything I can think of, with no joy. Comments have been made about your behaviour, you've been unusually antisocial and if you don't mind my saying so, you do seem a bit tense, so I do need to rule out drugs.... You can see that can't you?"

" No!" blurted Matt.
The major raised his eye brows.

"No, sir," Matt corrected himself. "I'm fed up with this fainting business and feel sick to the stomach about hurting someone, of course I am tense... Wouldn't you be? Yes you can have your sample, but you're wasting your time."

He had to concentrate hard to stop himself shaking. He felt bruised and battered from his fall, but he wasn't going to let anything show.

"I do hope so," agreed the doctor...

There was a tap on the door. An orderly came in with a tray holding two mugs of tea and a sample jar. Matt picked up the jar and headed for the toilet with it. A few moments later he returned and placed the full container back on the tray. He picked up his tea and returned to his seat.

The doctor picked the sample up and placed it in a clear plastic bag. "Thank you. This will take a couple of hours I'm afraid. I have to send it off to hospital for analysis and wait for them to get back to us. It can take a while if it's not urgent. "

"It's not urgent to me sir, I already know the result." Matt knew he was bordering on insolence, but he was so wound up he didn't care.

The major chose to ignore the comment. He stood up to leave the room. "Enjoy your tea, I will be back when I have the result. In the meantime though, you are not to leave the medical centre. Do you understand?"

" Yes sir." Matt wanted to say more about the fact that the doctor should be finding out what was really wrong rather than wasting time on drugs tests, but he knew this was not the time.

It took three hours for the results to come back. Matt was vaguely irritated that the doctor expected him to be pleased with the result. He had known what it would be. He was more interested in what was going to be happening next.

The Major on the other hand was visibly more relaxed, now that he wasn't dealing with a felon. He sat down next to Matt to explain the situation from the Navy's point of view. He spoke quickly; this was not going to be a discussion.

"I don't know what is wrong with you, but it is obvious that something isn't right, so I am going to refer you to a consultant. In the mean time however, we do not have the facilities to keep you safe here. Moreover, as this morning proved, I need to keep others safe around you. I am therefore going to send you home on sick leave. I will email your GP and set up the referral for as soon as I can. I take it that you would want to see somebody in Scotland? You pack your kit. I am assigning someone to escort you at all times. You will have a rail warrant for tomorrow morning."

Matt closed his eyes and breathed in deeply. He couldn't argue with the logic of what was being said although he was not happy about having a shadow. Home did sound appealing though, maybe space to sort himself out would be a good thing after all.

The Doctor was busy typing into an electronic tablet. He looked up. "What is the nearest train station to your home?" he asked.

Matt had heard this question before; it was obvious the Doctor hadn't read his file that well. "There isn't one, sir."

The Doctor sighed, he had hoped that the captain wasn't going to be difficult. "C'mon lad, there must be."

Matt didn't even look up at him. "Check the file. The nearest Station is Glasgow sir, then you fly to Benbecula, then drive to South Uist. There is a causeway between the two islands. Will the escort be coming all the way, Sir?"

"I'll get the travel sergeant to sort it then," muttered the doctor as he stood up. You just get yourself ready."

The arrangements were made. Matt contacted his family to tell them he was coming home for a couple of weeks. He didn't say why. He would explain what he could, when he got there. His sister Iona agreed to pick him up from the airport. He would arrive on the afternoon flight. His escort would accompany him to Glasgow airport, after which Flybe airline staff would look after him. There was the suggestion that they would provide a wheelchair too for him to board and depart the plane, but Matt refused this point blank. The airport staff were extremely helpful. They had obviously been briefed that he was unwell; Matt felt that they were assuming that it was somehow, "in the line of duty." He wasn't going to tell them what was wrong, but at the same time he felt a fraud every time one of them gave him a supportive look, or went out of their way to help him.

They sat Matt near the front left on one of the single window seats. It was a smooth flight on a bright afternoon. Matt leant his head against the window and closed his eyes. People often chatted on the small plane. Locals catching up or curious about visitors to their islands but Matt didn't want to make small talk with anyone.

Instinctively, he opened his eyes just as the Uists came into sight. He couldn't help but smile at the chain of shining gems, glittering in the turquoise sea. Home. Their natural beauty warmed his soul, like nowhere else on earth, as it always did. Everything was surely going to be OK.

Chapter Two

The cabin crew insisted that Matt was the last to leave the aircraft. Looking out of the window, Matt could see a man stood poised with a wheel chair at the aircraft steps. While he would put up with letting everyone go first, there was no way he was getting into that. The news that he was crippled in some way would reach his mother before he even got home. He strode purposefully past the chair across the tarmac to the small airport building. It was a converted RAF base from the 1950's and despite efforts to modernise it, still had the same functional demeanour. The man with the wheel chair followed him. It was only a short walk but to Matt it took an age as he willed himself to stay upright and not pass out. He was not going to do that here. He could see his sister through the large windows. He gave her a cheery wave. She waved back but with a curious smile. She could see that something was not quite right.

Iona watched her brother as he crossed the tarmac. It wasn't that he was unsteady on his feet but more that he seemed to be concentrating on every step. Iona had just qualified as a social worker. Between her training and innate perception she could feel a knot developing in her stomach and knew that whatever it was, her brother needed her more than he would ever let on. As he finally walked into the small arrivals lounge, she stepped forward and wrapped her arms around him. He hugged her back. They stood for a moment, oblivious to the airport workers loading baggage onto the small carousel and locking the airside doors behind them. Matt felt stupidly safe cuddling his little sister. He realised how much he had missed her, his family and his home.

She could feel his tension. "Don't worry, you're home now. We'll look after you." She whispered in his ear.

Matt stepped back, still holding her shoulders and grinned from ear to ear. "And what makes you think that I need looking after!" he joked in mock indignation. "Don't you start analysing me the moment I step off the plane."

"Well, it might possibly have something to do with you coming home suddenly without an explanation. Or that you made that walk across the tarmac as if it were thin ice; or even just that dude who was following you with the wheel chair, dodging about ready to catch you, while you were ignoring him. You didn't even say thank you and that's not like you."

"Doh, busted!" Matt sighed. "It's no drama really. People making a fuss. But I'll explain when we get home. You know that I'm going to have to go through every detail with mum at least twice."

"You think you're only going to get away with telling her twice," Iona laughed. "C'mon then, your taxi awaits sir." Iona gave him a mock salute and started out to the car park. Matt picked up his bag and followed her out. Her little pink Fiesta was parked a few minutes' walk away from the terminal building. He threw his bag into the boot. "You really going to make me travel in this thing?" He laughed pointing at the butterflies stencilled on the boot. Iona was getting into the car. "You can always walk," she replied. He didn't respond, or come round to get into the passenger seat. She looked around but couldn't see him. Confused for a moment; "where's he gone now?" she thought. Then she noticed a man from the other side of the car park running towards the car.

Iona jumped out of her seat and ran to the back of the car. She almost tripped over Matt's feet. He was lying on his side in the parking bay. She dropped to her knees beside him. "Matt, can you hear me?" He was breathing, but didn't answer. She stroked his head. She quickly checked his body. There was no sign of bleeding. He began to stir. The man approached. "Is he all right? Do you want me to call an ambulance?"

"No," grunted the supine figure beside her. The man came closer.

"I saw him. He said something, then just sort of collapsed. He didn't go down hard, but didn't move. Gave me one hell of a fright. You sure you're OK mate?"

Matt began to turn slowly round.

"Don't get up." Iona warned and put her hand on his chest.

Matt eased back and closed his eyes for a second. "It is OK. Just give me a minute and I will recover. Then we can go home. Believe me, I know about this; it's happened before."

"But..." interrupted Iona.

"No, the hospital won't find anything wrong. Nobody has before. They did all the checks down south. I'm just over tired."

A couple of people from the airport were heading towards them. "Help me up mate. I don't want to be a spectacle."

The man and Iona helped Matt to his feet and into the car. Iona felt very uneasy, but she knew her brother. Well if you still feel unwell when we get home, I'm bringing you straight back."

"I feel better already." He gave a weak smile.

Iona humphed as she started the car. "Well let's see what mum has to say."

"Don't tell her the minute we walk in. I'll explain everything. Don't want to worry her."

"Ok, but you certainly scared the shit out of me. She'll want you to go and get checked out."

"I have been, several times, believe me. I'm waiting to see a specialist. "

They didn't speak for the rest of the journey, both lost in their own thoughts.

About twenty minutes later the little pink fiesta adorned with multicolour butterflies pulled up outside the family home. Seonag had seen them coming down the road. "Well you can't miss her in that car really," she mused. She had the front door open and the kettle on. She was taking a tray of freshly baked scones out of the oven as she heard the car doors open and close.

Seonag sensed that something was wrong. Like Iona she had wondered about his sudden arrival. She could see that Matt was a bit subdued and Iona looked tense. She dreaded what he might have to tell her. Nevertheless, kisses and hugs were exchanged and tea and scones duly consumed around the kitchen table. The familiarity and smells of home felt good. Both women waited for Matt to tell his story.

As Matt started to talk he surprised himself at just how emotional he felt. He was frustrated and angry. Angry at the Navy, at the doctors, but most of all at himself. He wanted to be getting on with what he was good at and he hated not being in control.

His mother and sister listened without interruption.

"So they said they would notify the Doctors here?" She confirmed when he had finished.

Matt nodded.

"And they gave you no timescales for this specialist or didn't say what he would be a specialist in either." Seonag was thinking aloud.

Iona lent forward and took her brother's hand. "If they have found nothing physically wrong, it could just be stress or over work. You do go at one hundred and ten percent at everything. Maybe a bit of rest is the answer."

"But I don't feel stressed. I wasn't stressed in the airport car park, quite the opposite. It doesn't make sense," Matt moaned.

She squeezed his hand. "The brain doesn't work quite like that though. That's why they call it post traumatic... your body reacts after the event, just when you think everything is better. That is part of the cruelty of it."

Matt took his hand away. "I know about PTSD. I've seen people with it. I'm not convinced."

"And you've had no other symptoms?" his sister persisted.

Matt paused. "No." How could he explain feelings that he didn't understand?

Iona noted the pause, but didn't comment on it.

Seonag broke the impasse by offering more tea. "Well, I think you should give them a few days to send through whatever it is they're going to send, then go see Doctor Simpson and talk it through. After all, she's known you since you were a bairn. In the meantime just take it easy and we'll look after you. You never know, you might just need a rest."

"And try not to break anything when you fall down!" His sister added.

"I'll try." Matt smiled. Despite everything, his mother's practical approach made him feel better. He knew that she would be panicking inside, but that she and his sisters would always be there for him.

For the next few days everyone, including Matt was on tenterhooks. Everyone was just waiting for him to pass out again. His mother and sister tried not to let him be alone for too long; shouted through the door when he was in the bathroom and refused point blank to let him drive. He was beginning to feel cooped up. But on the positive side he didn't pass out. Perhaps his mum had been right. A fortnight later he still hadn't got round to making that appointment with Dr. Simpson. When his Commanding Officer rang to see how he was getting on, he was happy to tell him that there was nothing to report. They agreed that he should still wait to see the specialist before he returned to work, but planned for that to be sooner rather than later. His family relaxed and didn't feel the need to be quite so vigilant. Matt began to feel he could enjoy life again; perhaps he could start going out and about and actually enjoy the chance to spend some time at home.

It was just before the late May bank holiday, Seonag was planning to spend the long weekend with a friend on Skye and Iona had been invited to a beach party on the little island of Berneray at the top of North Uist.

"Why don't you come with me?" She suggested to Matt. "It's just a bunch of people from school who are home for the holiday. There's going to be a BBQ and music, we are camping on the beach."

Matt was tempted, but not sure. He didn't like the idea that she was babysitting him. "You won't want me to be hanging round with you and your school mates."

"On the contrary, neither Iain nor Kate can get back from work on the mainland and I'm going to need help putting my tent up. The forecast doesn't look all that great so I'm going to need some brawn. Besides, you'll know a lot of them. Robbie's big sister, Rhona is going to be there. You'll enjoy the chance to let your hair down."

Matt understood his sister. He knew that she was missing her fiancé Iain. As a child she and her twin sister were inseparable, so perhaps, deep down, she just didn't like turning up to places by herself. He also remembered Rhona. She had been in the year below him at school. A bit of a wild child with vividly coloured hairstyles, he remembered. Attractive too. It could be fun.

"Whereabouts are you going?"

"The north end. By the youth hostel, You know where the rocky bit and the beach meet. The plan is to camp on the machair by the dunes. Then if it does get a bit wild we can always retire to the hostel."

Matt considered the rocky east coast more interesting than just camping on the beach, but suspected that he would be in the minority.

He looked at his sister as she busied herself around the kitchen. He just needed to be sure that it wasn't a sympathy invitation. Despite having her back to him, she could feel his gaze.

"This is on the basis that you are really as better as you look." She said over her shoulder. "I won't be dragging you up that beach if you pass out on me."

"Yes you would." Matt laughed. "God, the thought of you and Rhona taking an arm and leg each is enough to keep a man on his feet!"

"Ha! I knew Rhona would be a consideration," she teased. "So you're coming then?"

Matt agreed and they made their plans. He did feel better and was looking forward to the weekend. But that night in bed he couldn't shake off an uneasy sense of foreboding.

Chapter Three

The Friday Bank Holiday morning was a busy one. Seonag left early to catch the ferry from Lochmaddy to Uig on the Isle of Skye. She was glad to see her son relaxed and doing things again. She hoped that this marked the beginning of his recovery and felt that she had to give him space to get back on his feet again.

Iona and Matt packed their car around lunch time. The boot and back seat were crammed with tents, bedding and supplies. When they stopped at the Co-op for even more food, Matt teased her that he normally only went out with his back pack and rations. She was buying enough for a small siege, not just a night on the beach.

"You can't have enough chocolate and rum," she maintained, "especially if it's going to be cold and wet. It's not poor weather that stops you...It's poor preparation!"

He couldn't argue with her there, so just loaded the shopping bags into the car as they set off to pick up Rhona.

Since their original conversation, Iona had arranged to pick up her friend. It made sense as she did not drive and lived on Grimsay, which was on their way. Matt did wonder if his sister was match making. He decided that it was unlikely, but then again, he didn't mind if she was.

Rhona, by contrast jumped into the car carrying only a big handbag and a bottle of vodka. She was a tall, long legged girl, with short cropped, bright orange hair and piercing green eyes. Dressed in black skinny jeans and a loose khaki jacket, swaddled in an over sized orange scarf. A cross between Che Guevara and Mother Theresa, Matt thought. But it somehow suited her, with her easy smile and attitude to take on the world.

She squeezed into the back seat, moving the shopping bags. "My God "I", where we going with this lot? You expecting to feed the five thousand?"

"Hush! You'll thank me at three o'clock in the morning!" Iona retorted.

The laughing and banter continued as they journeyed north. Rhona was not aware that Matt had been ill, she just thought that he was home on leave and was curious about the places he'd been and what he'd been up to. Matt felt good being treated normally again.

There were a couple of lads already putting up tents when they arrived in Berneray. Matt vaguely recognised them, but didn't know them. Introductions were made and they set about preparing. Matt and the girls put up a two man tent and a single tent. The wind was coming from the east, blowing onto the sea, stirring up white horses. They pitched the tents close to the steep bank of dunes that separated the beach from the machair.

Music was provided from someone's car, a fire pit was dug in the sand and soon lit. Bags of food piled up ready to be cooked as a BBQ. More people arrived, some stayed, others went. There were not as many as originally expected. People milled around and chatted. As the afternoon wore on, Matt admitted to himself that he was really quite bored. He wasn't in the mood for socialising, but Iona seemed to be enjoying herself, so he didn't mind that much. They had all had a drink, so they were there for the night. Matt sat down next to his tent and sipped his beer. It was a good spot. The heat from the fire was just enough to keep the chill away and he had a clear view of the sun setting through the clouds onto the turbulent water. He used to watch the sunsets with his dad when they were fishing. "Always look out for the green flash," his dad had told him. Wouldn't see one with this cloud, It's getting worse, he thought. Or did someone say that? He looked around, but nobody was close. As the sun descended the sky darkened to a heavy slate grey. The wind was getting up, spitting the odd shard of rain against his face.

"Looks like the weather has put peeps off," Rhona complained nosily as she plonked herself down next to Matt, supping from a bottle. "I don't blame them really," he responded.

"White laits!" she slurred.

Matt looked at her, confused for a second. "You mean light weights?"

"Aye that's what I said."

"Think you're the white lait to be pished so soon." He laughed. Glad to have Rhona to lighten his mood.

"Me pished? Fie on you man! Just having a good time. Eat drink and be merry!"

"Talking about food, have you eaten? I didn't see anything being cooked." He noticed that several of the bags of food had disappeared.

Rhona followed his gaze. "They've taken it to cook in the hostel. Reckoned it's too windy to put it on the fire."

Matt took her arm. "Well, I think we should go and join them and get some food inside you."

"Oh Mr. Macaulay, you taking me to dinner?"

"C'mon," he laughed, it'll be good to get out of the wind anyway."

"Ah, how romantic."

Matt half pulled, half coaxed Rhona up through the dunes. They stumbled across the grass towards the hostel which was about fifteen yards away. A short stroll in the daylight, it took longer under the now blackening sky, pushing against the wind.

The hostel was an old, whitewashed, stone building with a thatched roof. The heavy front door opened into a dimly lit corridor. On the right was a kitchen. He could hear Iona laughing in there. From the sounds and the smells she was cooking, part of him wanted to go in and talk to her; to tell her how he was feeling. But how was he feeling? Don't be selfish, he thought, you can't ruin her night just because you are feeling a bit left out. Is that what was wrong? Rhona made his mind up for him. "Don't go in there, they'll only find us something to do... this way, follow me." She took his hand. "How long is it since you've been here? You look a bit lost."

She led the way through the door on the left into the bunk room. Bunk beds lined the walls, jammed in between well worn sofas and a small table. The room was dark and crowded. The music blared, so much so that people were shouting to be heard above it. The musky smell of weed hung in the air.

"You probably won't approve of this," Rhona shouted in his ear," but hang on and I'll be back in a mo."

Before he could reply Rhona was clumsily making her way across the room to a furtive huddle, Matt suspected was the source of the distinctive smell. He could see that people were getting annoyed as she fell into them. He wondered what the chances were of her making it back.

"Look at you, what a loser." The voice sounded cruel and harsh. Matt looked around to see who had spoken, but those around him were all engrossed in their own conversations.

"You don't belong here. You don't belong in the navy. Your family are too busy for you. What a joke." It was a male mocking voice that sounded horribly familiar, but Matt couldn't place it.

"Fuck off!" He retorted. He obviously spoke louder than he had thought, as several people turned to look at him.

Matt scoured the room, but he had a horrible sensation that he knew where the voice was coming from. "Who are you?" he demanded.

"Your worst nightmare." The voice growled, then started laughing. It had a steely tone.

Matt shook his head, but he couldn't stop the laughing. It was cold and incessant.

He was more scared than he had ever been before. He didn't understand what was happening. He gripped his head in his hands but he couldn't stop the laughing.

He was aware that more people were staring at him. Some were sniggering and making comments. But he couldn't see anyone laughing. This could not be happening.

Rhona had noticed that something was wrong and was heading back across the room towards him. While she could be hedonistic and appear out for a good time, she could recognise a troubled soul and knew she had to help.

"Don't talk to her. She'll think you're mad." The voice barked. "Get out."

Matt didn't want to obey the voice, but he felt he had no choice. "Iona," he mumbled.

"No!" snapped the voice. "She's a Social worker. She will have you locked up. Then you will really be fucked."

The voice played to Matt's worst fears. He had no choice. He turned, fumbled with the door, but managed to get it open. In the cool, quieter hall he could hear Iona's voice and felt a little better. But there were people with her. He had to get outside.

Matt gulped the cold air greedily as he lurched through the hostel door into the night. It felt good. He ran across the grass bounding over the fence onto the machair without missing a heartbeat. He just wanted to get away, a primitive urge to flee.

He didn't even notice the dunes underfoot as he descended into the sand. He pounded onto the beach, past the remains of the fire towards the water line. The sand became firmer against his pounding feet. He wasn't thinking about where he was going. He didn't even see the ocean in front of him.

A sudden noise broke through his consciousness. A desperate keening, wailing sound. He paused, someone was calling his name. He turned around and strained to focus back along the shore line. The slight figure of a woman was unsteadily making her way down through the dunes.

She looked up and saw that he had stopped. She waved frantically. "Matt, wait for me!" She called. Suddenly the voice was back, clearer than before.

" Run away... She's not your friend! She was laughing at you."

"No she wasn't," argued Matt. She is my friend."

"She will have been giggling with Iona while you are out here in the cold," the voice sneered.

"No!" shouted Matt. "Iona wouldn't do that." He was close to tears with rage and frustration. He was desperate to think straight but logic eluded him.

Rhona made her way gingerly onto the beach. She couldn't understand what was happening. She could see Matt a little way away, he was standing in the shallows, oblivious to the waves splashing his legs and feet, arguing with somebody. But there was nobody else there. She ran towards him as fast as she could, adrenalin nullifying the alcohol in her system.

Slowing to a walking place, Rhona tried to appear nonchalant as she approached. "Hey ya, you not getting wet? Do you want to come back to the fire? It was a bit much inside wasn't it?" She held out her hands and slowly stepped towards him.

Matt desperately wanted to take her hands, but the voice was shouting at him. He couldn't understand what it was saying, but the loud angry noise was blocking his thoughts and his ability to speak. He turned away in an attempt to appease it and quiet it somehow.

Rhona was terrified. She was scared that he would run into the sea. She had to think quickly. If she tried to grab him they could both fall into the water, he was bigger and stronger than her. Still trying to appear light hearted she unwrapped her scarf from around her neck. Holding both ends she quietly moved closer until she was just arms' length away. The water was lapping her feet too, but he seemed oblivious to her. In a swift movement she threw the scarf over his head, it landed around his chest.

As if suddenly awakened, he immediately freed his arms and turned toward her. The voice was screaming at him to rip it off, he knew he could. He looked at her as she held the ends of the scarf firmly and felt somehow reassured. "It's OK Matt. I've got you." She spoke quietly. "Let's go find Iona. Would you like to do that?"

He nodded. Moving slowly, Rhona took a step backwards. He followed. He was holding onto the scarf too, gripping hard with both hands, willing himself to follow her and ignore the voice. He would be safe with Iona. They didn't speak. Maintaining eye contact they inched across the sand away from the water line.

Their concentration was abruptly interrupted by a figure on the dunes. "Matt, Matt, I'm coming!" It was Iona.

Matt looked up, strangely reassured to hear her. He found his voice and called her name in reply.

But this didn't reassure Iona. She heard the pain and desperation in his voice. She had to get to him. In the dark, she was concentrating on the two figures on the sand. She went to run towards them but missed her footing. She shrieked as her ankle gave way under her, sending her toppling through the marram grass and landing with a thud on the sand.

"She's alright," Rhona assured Matt as she watched her friend pull herself up. But her relief was short lived as she felt her scarf being pulled out of her hands. Matt had dropped to the ground beside her unconscious, face down on the sand.

Despite the grinding pain in her leg, Iona was at her brother's side as he came round. Both girls sat with him on the sand as he pulled himself together. He said nothing for a moment. He looked as if he was concentrating hard, then gave a weak smile. "I feel better actually. I think it's gone."

Iona was confused and was about to ask what had gone, but stopped when Rhona shook her head at her. "I'm sorry Matt, we shouldn't have come. I guess you're not as recovered as we thought you were. Do you want to go back inside?"

She was a little taken aback when both he and Rhona both replied with a firm no. But then remembered some of the comments being made that her brother had been acting strangely which had prompted her to come and look for him.

The rain had stopped and the wind had dropped away. The moon was still hidden by a heavy layer of clouds, but it looked as if the storm had passed. They decided that the best thing to do was to settle down in their tent for the night. This time Matt supported his sister as they hobbled back up the beach. He wanted to carry her, but she wouldn't let him. They found some dry wood and revived the fire. Rhona volunteered to go back into the hostel to find them some food. While she was gone Matt managed to tell Iona a little of what had happened. She held him close while he spoke, trying to make sense of what he was saying.

"But it's gone completely now you say?"

"Yes, maybe it was the beer, I don't know."

Iona knew that a couple of bottles of Becks was hardly lightly to send her brother into such a state, but didn't comment. Eventually Rhona returned with some food. She explained that she had reassured people that Matt was ok now and that most were putting it down to the "deoch." He wasn't overly pleased by that, and even less by the fact that she had returned with three veggie burgers. Noticing his expression, Iona laughed. "Well you did come camping with two vegetarians." She rummaged in the tent and produced a Co-op bag full of goodies. "I told you that you would thank me for this." She laughed as Matt pulled out bags of crisps and sausage rolls.

They decided that the three of them would sleep together in the same tent. They strapped Iona's ankle as best they could and Rhona's and Matt's feet had dried a little by the fire. Despite the dull thud of a base line emanating from the hostel, it was not long before the three of them were snuggled up asleep under a pile of sleeping bags.

Matt opened his eyes, his head felt fuzzy. He couldn't work out where he was or what he was looking at. The gentle snoring from one of the girls reminded him where he was. Horrible memories from the night before came flooding back. But he was still confused. Why was the sky so bright through the canvas? Surely it was still night. The answer came in a loud roar as thunder suddenly resounded around their small tent. It was the opening crescendo, bringing with it torrential rain that pelted the side of the tent and a ferocious wind that rocked the frame.

The girls stirred. "What's going on?" murmured Iona half sitting up.

It was the voice that answered. "It's the storm you idiot! You thought it had passed, but it was only the eye, now it's come back with a vengeance. You should have known Macaulay! You're responsible for this. You're all going to die and it's your fault."

"No!" Shouted Matt. "Leave me alone".

Both girls were wide awake now. They were freaked more by the fact that Matt was arguing with himself than they were by the storm.

"Let's get to the Hostel," suggested Iona, putting her arm around her brother's shoulder.

"Ha! They'll all laugh at you there," sneered the voice. "They'll know what a failure you are. What a brave marine who can't protect two girls from the weather."

"No." Matt growled this time. Shaking his sister off.

Rhona didn't know why, but she had seen how he had been in the hostel earlier, so agreed that she didn't think the hostel was a good idea. "What about the car, could you make it up there Iona?"

Matt remembered his sister's twisted ankle and felt even guiltier. He was angry at the voice because deep down he felt that it was right. He had got them into this mess.

The girls were scrambling into their shoes and jackets in the cramped space. "C'mon Matt put your shoes on," coaxed his sister. "We'll get the heater on in the car."

Matt didn't answer but he did pull his trainers on. He crawled forward and unzipped the tent. The flaps blew back and smacked across his face. The wind and sand swirled in, taking all their breath away. He stumbled out and braced himself against the wind. It took all his strength to remain upright against the elements. He tried to lean on the tent, but with the force of the storm behind him it distorted under his weight. The lightning crackled menacingly close overhead. He could see the debris from the remains of the party swirling towards them. He leant in and offered his arm to Iona. She tried to stand up, but her ankle gave way beneath her. She yelped with the pain, but knew she had to keep going. Rhona pushed her from behind and she fell into her brother's arms.

Matt was aware that the voice was still with him, but while he concentrated on helping his sister he was managing to keep it at bay. Rhona scrambled out swearing under her breath as she clung onto the other two. They had all grown up with the Hebridean weather but this was different. Nobody said it, but they were all terrified.

Their clothes were sodden within seconds of standing on the beach. They clung onto each other, hardly able to see as the sand was blown into their eyes. It was painful even to look up as the slicing rain smarted as it cut into their skin. Turning inland, at least the wind was behind them.

Matt's survival instinct took over. He and Rhona supported Iona between them. The forlorn looking trio slowly made their way towards safety. Clambering through the dunes was an ordeal. The sand shifted under their feet. It felt like two steps forward and three steps back. Rhona led the way, but her slight frame was blown over several times, slipping back onto Matt who was by now virtually carrying Iona. Matt used his body weight to hold the three of them steady. At times he couldn't see and his head swam. His hands were cut and bleeding by the sharp, wet marram grass, but he did not feel it. They had to keep going.

Rhona finally fell over the top of the dune on to the blessed sheep cropped grass. She turned and pulled Iona up, Matt staggering close behind. It wasn't far to the car, but now, higher up, they were more exposed and the wind took on a greater intensity. They could hardly breathe. Heads down, half standing, half crawling, they battled their way towards the car. The wind direction felt as if it was changing with every step. Lightning split the sky again and the thunder roared angrily. But in the sharp flashes of light they could see the car slowly growing closer. When they reached the vehicle they rested, leaning against it for a moment, catching their breath. It rocked ominously in the wind.

"I'll get the door, you two jump in the back," Matt had to shout to make himself heard.

He pulled open the door with both hands. The wind caught it and pushed it hard against him. He felt the hinges strain as he fought to keep hold of it. The girls fell into the back, pulling the passenger back rest behind them. Matt, still holding the door, fell into the front seat, pulling his legs in, he gave the door an almighty yank. It didn't catch on the first attempt, but he managed on his second try. They had made it.

Nobody spoke. The car rocked. The rain was hammering against the windows. There was no sense of relief. Cold and wet, Matt exhaled in a long painful gasp. Both girls were sobbing quietly.

" Think you're clever do you? What you going to do now boy wonder?" The voice sneered in Matt's head.

" Just fuck off will ya!" Matt snapped.

The voice laughed.

Matt wrapped his arms around his head and started rocking in the seat. He was sobbing now. "Leave me alone, just leave me alone!" The voice just kept coldly laughing, resonating in his head.

Iona lent forward and put her hand on her brother's shoulder.

" This is what he was like earlier," Rhona whispered.

" They think you're mad," the voice taunted. "They'll have you locked up... Your own family too."

" For fuck's sake, leave me alone!" Growled Matt.

Iona withdrew her hand slightly.

Matt took hold of it. "No, not you, don't leave me."

She squeezed his hand.

" Never Matt, I'm here. You just saved me we're going to get through this."

Matt took her hand with both of his hands and snuggled up to it like a small boy. She talked quietly to him. He was lost in his own thoughts, but seemed calmer.

The wind had abated slightly although it was still raining heavily. Rhona rummaged in her pockets and pulled out her mobile phone.

"Believe it or not, I have signal."

"Who are you going to call at this time of night?" asked Iona.

"it's three AM. You can't drive, cos you've had a drink and your ankle, your brother is seriously unwell and we may all have pneumonia. The only person I can, Aunty Joan."

Iona had forgotten that their GP, Joan Simpson, was Rhona's aunt. "That ok with you Matt?" She asked quietly. He raised his head slightly. Their eyes met and he gave a slight nod.

Rhona made the call.

Chapter Four

Dr. Joan Simpson had practised medicine in the Hebrides for about thirty years, when asked, she would tell people that she had lost count. She arrived in Benbecula as a newly qualified locum in 1984 and fell in love, firstly with her new island home and then with her husband Jordan Campbell. She was always known as Dr. Simpson rather than by her married name. She was a tall angular woman, who never quite managed elegance, but her open enthusiasm for life and infectious laugh won her a place in the hearts of the locals that made her trusted and respected.

She wasn't on duty over the bank holiday weekend, but out of habit she was attuned to hearing the phone in the middle of the night. She was tempted to turn over and ignore it, but curiosity got the better of her. When she saw that it was Rhona and realised the time, she was suddenly wide awake. She sat up and took the call.

After a few minutes she simply said. "Ok, I'll be there." Her niece had spoken quickly, with quiet intensity. There were questions to be asked, but they could wait till she got there.

" Make sure you turn on the car headlights so that I can see you." She put down the phone and nudged her husband.

"I'm just going up to Berneray to pick up Rhona and a couple of her friends who are in a bit of trouble. I will be about an hour, I hope."

"Are you mad woman? Have you heard it out there? I've no sympathy if she's got drunk and doesn't want to face her mother. She's a grown woman now."

"No, she's with the Macaulay kids. Iona has had some sort of accident and Matt, you remember, the Marine, is unwell. Seonag is away, so they are a bit stuck. We're only half an hour away. I think I ought to go."

Jordan knew that he couldn't talk his wife out of going really."Do you want me to come? That's a dangerous road on a night like this."

"I'm Ok," she smiled as she started to get dressed. "I'm used to it."

What she didn't mention was that she had recently read the referral letter from the military medics about Matt. She was concerned by fact that he was arguing with himself and sounded as if he was losing it as Rhona had described it. He needed someone that he knew and hopefully trusted.

Joan lived near the old harbour in Lochmaddy. Her house was an old Victorian building that once belonged to the Granville Estate which owned North Uist. It was draughty, but built to withstand the elements. Joan decided to turn the heating on the Aga up before she left, as she felt it might be a long night. It was normally a twenty minute drive over to Berneray, but the road was twisty and exposed. As she turned off the main road she half wished she had taken Jordan up on his offer.

Following the twisty road from Lochmaddy to Berneray Joan ran through in her mind what she was likely to find. Rhona could be a drama queen, but her account had an uncanny ring of authenticity about it. Joan was worried. It felt as if her car had to push against the elements as she crossed the small causeway to the northerly island. The Leverburgh ferry, which was moored next to the causeway, rocked as if weightless, ominously close to the road. Joan made a mental note to let the Coastguard know. They might want to check it out.

She followed the coast road heading towards the youth hostel. It was very dark and she wondered if they had lost power; it happened frequently during storms. Eventually she spotted the car lights in the distance. She was glad of them, otherwise she would have missed the turn onto the track for the hostel.

She pulled up next to Iona's Fiesta, facing into the wind. Flinging her medical bag over her shoulder, and using both hands, it took all her strength to push her car door open. It was an effort, but she would rather that than the wind blowing the door off its hinges. That had happened all too often before. Steadying herself on the car, she made her way around the front to the driver's door. She waited a minute for a pause between the gusts, then pulled the door open and flopped in beside Matt. He looked up but didn't speak. He was still holding onto Iona.

"It's a bit wild out there isn't it?" Joan spoke as if it was totally normal for her to be getting into a car in the middle of the night. Talking directly to Matt, she quietly explained why she was there. "Rhona called me because she was worried about Iona's ankle and said that you were not feeling too well. Is that right?"

Matt nodded slightly.

"Ok, well, just let me speak to Iona about her injury, then well, perhaps I should drive us all back to my house, the kitchen is nice and toasty, so we can get you all dried off and have a chat, ok?"

Matt squeezed Iona's hand tightly. The voice was raging at him again. "NO! NO! NO! Don't trust her, she'll say you are mad and lock you away. Get out, they'll never catch you."

Matt turned towards Iona. In the half light he could see her give him an encouraging smile, he also saw her wincing in pain as she must have moved her leg. He braced himself, he had to ignore the voice. "I do, I do, I do trust her," he repeated to himself.

He noticed Iona change position. He hadn't realised that the doctor had been talking to her. She had moved to sit sideways and lift her leg onto Rhona's lap. She cried out at the movement, but didn't let go of her brother.

Joan didn't want to linger, she was thankful that like most people in Uist, Iona had left her car keys in the ignition. She started the engine. "Let's go and get a nice cup of tea."

The drive back was easier with the wind behind them. When they arrived back at the house Joan asked Matt if he could help Iona into the house. She was slightly taken aback when he picked her up and carried her lightly in his arms. Joan opened the front door for them and Rhona followed behind. As she shut the door Joan gave her niece a quick hug. "Thanks for calling me, you did the right thing."

They went through a wide, tiled hall into a cosy kitchen with a large table and an Aga on one side.

"Rhona, put the kettle on. Matt, put Iona down here."

Joan removed Iona's trainer and examined her foot. She was fairly sure that it was not broken, but it was bruising badly. She bound it up and after confirming how much alcohol Iona had drunk, gave her some painkillers. Rhona had made tea and found biscuits. Matt hadn't touched his; he was just looking at it intently. Sitting down next to Matt, Joan asked him quietly, "Is it ok if the girls tell me what happened tonight?" After a moment, his eyes still fixed on his tea, he nodded slightly.

Between them the girls told the story. Iona asked if the Navy had contacted her about Matt, but Joan didn't answer, she didn't want anything to stress or worry Matt even more. As they spoke Joan gently stroked the back of Matt's hand. When they had finished she said nothing for a moment.

"Sounds like you are having an awful time, even for someone like you who has faced danger all around the world."

He didn't respond.

"We've known each other for a long time haven't we? When you had glandular fever, all those knocks and scrapes as a teenager; You even let me cut out your ingrown toenail. Do you remember?"

Matt gave a slight smile.

"You know that all I want to do is help you feel better. You know that don't you?" she gave his hand a slight squeeze.

It took a minute. Matt's eyes were darting round the room. His shoulders stiffened, but he finally nodded slowly.

"I'd like to ask you a couple of questions to find out what's wrong. Do you want Rhona and Iona to leave?"

This time he shook his head quickly. He wasn't so bothered what Rhona did, but he did not want to be separated from his sister.

"Ok," Joan continued gently. "Iona says that you told her that you are hearing a voice in your head. Is that right?"

Matt couldn't answer at first. He barely had space in his head for his own thoughts. The voice was shouting, screaming, banging. Matt had to use all his strength to push it back.

"Yes," he muttered.

"Ok," replied Joan calmly. "Now, I need to reassure you, this happens to a lot of people." Matt looked at her for the first time.

"Honestly, I treat far more people than you would think for this sort of thing. It often goes away after treatment, or can be managed. So try not to worry." She paused to let him take this in.

"I can give you some medicine that will make it go away for now and let you get some sleep. Would you like me to get you some?"

Matt didn't reply.

"You will get some rest, then after the weekend we can arrange for you to see a specialist to get things sorted properly. What do you think?" She urged.

The voice was still objecting violently, screaming obscenities about Matt, the doctor and his family. Oddly, matt felt offended by this, but mostly he just wanted to sleep and block this all out. He nodded slowly again.

"Good," Smiled Joan. "I will just go and sort them out. I am not the doctor on call tonight, so I have to call the duty doctor to let him know what I am giving you."

Matt sat upright, suddenly very tense. "See! Fucking told you!" Screamed the voice. "She's lying! She is going to call the police to take you away. Get out of here." The obscenities continued.

"You can listen if you like," Joan reassured him, I can ask him to send an email to the specialist too, so that it will be in his office first thing. Rhona, pass me the phone, I'll call from here and will you go and throw a duvet on the bed in the spare room for me."

Iona, sat on the other side of Matt and put her arm around his shoulder as Joan made the call. She put her head close and spoke quietly to him. She kept repeating that she loved him and that he was going to be alright. She was trying not to cry, but he could hear the emotion in her voice. He felt guilty at upsetting her, but reassured by her depth of feeling.

After a few moments Joan finished on the phone and turned to Matt again.

"Ok , I am going to give you a tablet called Haloperidol. It's what they call an antipsychotic. It will knock you out pretty quickly. But it will help till we can speak to the specialist and decide on something more specific. Ok?" Joan was keen that Matt was agreeing with his treatment: if she had to do something against his will it would have been a different matter.

They agreed that she would give the tablet to him in bed so that he could settle down to sleep. Joan raised concerns that Iona might not be able to make it upstairs, but Iona was determined that she was not going to leave her brother. For a second Matt looked as if he was about to carry her again, but Joan put him off saying that she was worried that he might pass out on the stairs carrying his sister. He reluctantly agreed.

Rhona helped Iona upstairs and found her a tee shirt to sleep in. Matt stripped down to his underwear. He fell asleep almost immediately after taking the tablet. Iona lay on the bed next to him. She dozed on and off but was wide awake before dawn.

At eight o'clock in the morning there was a tap on the door. It was Joan, with a cup of tea and Iona's dried clothes over her arm. "I'm making some breakfast, why don't you come and have some. You should probably ring your mum too."

Iona agreed. She looked across her brother, who hadn't stirred. "Don't worry about Matt, he will sleep for an hour or two yet. We can leave the door open, so we will hear him."

Iona made the calls to her mother and sister. The storm was abating, but the ferries were cancelled until later in the afternoon at the earliest.

When Matt finally awoke, he was quiet and listless. Joan gave him some more of the Haloperidol. He picked at his breakfast and only spoke when spoken to. Joan suggested that they stayed until Seonag got back. Jordan was dispatched to retrieve Joan's car. Rhona asked if they could watch a film. Joan agreed that was a good idea, so they settled down to watch an old favourite, Cool Runnings.

By the evening, Matt was feeling anxious again. Joan gave him some diazepam as well as the antipsychotic to help him to stay calm for the journey home.

Seonag arrived after nine. She was shocked to see her son, sitting vacantly staring into mid air. Joan explained what she had given him, and the referral that had to be made. It was just a matter of keeping him stable until they could see the psychiatrist. She would not speculate on what might be causing the hallucinations, but assured Seonag as best she could that people live everyday with similar conditions and that they could be managed.

They only waited a couple of weeks for the consultant appointment. But it was a long couple of weeks. Matt was either very anxious and shouting at the imaginary voice or lethargic, sitting staring into space. When he was anxious he had difficulty trusting or talking to his mum or Iona. When he was like that he would talk for ages to his sister Kate on the phone. His friend Stuart Steele would come round and they would go out on his motor bike, the exhilaration of which seemed to lift his mood.

When the consultant's appointment came around it was something and nothing. The psychiatrist was called Mr. Rogers and Matt had to travel to Inverness to see him, his mother and sister going with him. Matt got on with him very well and was able to talk candidly to him about what had happened, more than he had been able to with his family. Mr. Rogers felt that it was too early to give a diagnosis. He changed the medication to a drug called Risperdal, which he said would allow him to live more normally and booked an MRI scan. He also suggested a course of counselling. While none of them really expected an instant cure, they felt frustrated that they could not tie the doctor down to a prognosis. Worse news for Matt though, was the doctors view that it could be at least two years until he was better, whatever better was. His mother and sister tried to reassure him that at least he now had a time frame; this wasn't forever. But all he could see was his life and career disappearing in front of him. His mood was very dark.

Things got worse while they waited for the MRI Scan. Matt was passing out even more, often several times a day. He couldn't be left alone, he wasn't able to have a shower, but had to bath with someone sitting in the room on the other side of the shower curtain. Even with the drugs he was not able to sleep and became agitated at night. Dr. Joan suggested increasing the dosage of his medication, but he did not want that. They found that if his mind was occupied he was calmer. They came up with the old childhood habit of reading to him before he fell asleep. Seonag and Iona took it in turns to stay in his room with him and read aloud until he fell asleep. Sometimes he would wake in the night, so they just carried on reading until he slept again. The book of choice was Lord of the Rings. They worked their way through it.

Then one evening, just after dinner, Matt was staring intently at the kitchen door.

"What are you looking at?" his mother asked.

"Can't you see him?"

"No. Who is he?"

"There's a small boy. He's dirty. He looks lost and confused. He's scared."

Seonag told Dr. Joan and they changed the dosage of his medication, but the scared little boy did not leave him.

Matt was assigned a CPN who he saw regularly, the family never knew what they talked about, but when she suggested he tried meditation, he laughed at the idea at first, but Kate sent him a book on it and he began to practise the techniques. The CPN helped in other ways too. It took a while, but Matt did found himself talking about things that he hadn't realised had bothered him. He began to understand his own anger at not only being away for his father's death but the feeling of responsibility he then felt for his mother and his sisters. These clashed with his responsibilities as a Marine which took him away. Whatever he did he was letting somebody down. He had not thought about it like that before; he was at war with himself. It was suggested that this was a form of PTSD, the problem was that he didn't know how to stop it.

There was talk on a couple of occasions about him being admitted to hospital. Matt didn't want to go and Seonag was determined to look after her son at home as long as she could. She was heartbroken to see her once witty energetic young man being reduced to what at times seemed like a half life, but he was her son and she would do the best for him whatever.

Matt was determined not to give in to the voice. He told himself that he had fought worse than this and he too wanted his life back. The medication made it quieter, less insistent, but it was still there, but he would not be beaten. He found that when he was concentrating on things he felt better and did not pass out. He started to cook and bake. The more complicated the recipe the better. A friend who ran a local cafe was happy for him help in her kitchen. It got him out of the house for a couple of hours which was a boost for him and a rest for his family. By the time the appointment for the MRI came through the family had got into their own strange but manageable routine. Some people gave Matt sideways looks if they saw him about or made nasty remarks just out of earshot. Others dropped in or took the opportunity to tell Seonag or Iona that they or members of their family had been through something similar. It was as if mental illness was a dark secret thing that people didn't talk about out loud. Rhona and Stuart took him and Iona out and Kate came home as much as she could. They learned to laugh and live through the illness. The voice was referred to as "Figgy" as it was a figment of his imagination. His friends would join Matt in arguing with Figgy, which helped it be ok for Matt to talk about it and let others know when it was bad. He had good days and bad days. He wouldn't accept calls or suggested visits from friends from his unit because he couldn't stand the thought of them seeing him like this. When he was down, he felt very alone. It was just Matt and Figgy.

The appointment for the MRI scan was at the General Hospital in Glasgow it was mid morning on a Thursday so the family decided to make a break of it and take a few days on the mainland. Kate would come down from Fort William where she was working and join them afterwards.

The scan was itself was quite routine. Matt didn't like the noise or the confined space, but it was bearable. He got himself dressed and was looking forward to meeting up with Kate in TGI Friday for lunch.

Glasgow at the time was littered with road works and diversions. They had to follow their SatNav back into town. Kate, who was having the same difficulties coming from the north, rang a couple of times for directions and updates. When Matt's phone rang for a third time, Matt answered it with a terse "for goodness sake girl, are you lost again?"

It was a male voice that replied sounding a little taken aback. "Is that Mr. Macaulay?"

"Yes", Matt replied, "who is this?"

"Ehm, this is staff nurse Johnson from the General radiological department. You had an MRI with us this morning. Are you still in Glasgow?"

Matt confirmed that he was.

"We are wondering if it would be possible for you to come back."
Matt felt alarmed. His sister and mother were straining to hear the conversation.

"Why?"

"Well, hem, the thing is we, er, didn't manage to do it properly, so as you are still here and have travelled so far, we thought you might be able to pop back and we can take another one."

Matt told his sister and mother what had been said and they agreed to go back. Matt explained that they might be a while because of the road works. Nurse Johnson told them not to worry but to come straight in when they got there.

They were all slightly bemused. It wasn't normal to be called back to a hospital like that, but they had come this far so it was the only sensible option. They rang Kate and delayed lunch.

When they got back to the radiological department there was nobody waiting and they were ushered straight in. It seemed a little less formal than the earlier appointment had been and took longer. While they were waiting a nurse came in with a big carrier bag full of sandwiches and drinks. She went into the control room where the staff were operating the MRI machine. She had left the door slightly ajar.

"Mum, they are handing round crisps and sandwiches while they are doing Matt's MRI," whispered Iona. "I'm not sure that's right you know."

Seonag looked at her watch. "Well, it is lunchtime."

They looked at each other, sharing the same thought. "They don't normally call you back and work through their lunch break do they?"

"No sweetie, I've never known it before."

The conversation was interrupted by Nurse Johnson coming back into the waiting room. "Won't be long now," she told them breezily.

"Is everything Ok", asked Seonag. "You guys are working through your lunch break."

The nurse assured them that all was fine; they were just concerned that they hadn't done it properly earlier and didn't want to drag them all the way back from the islands.

This somehow didn't ring true to the two women especially as the nurse hadn't made eye contact while she was talking.

A good if late lunch was had and little more was said about the nurses' lunchtime shift. They visited the Falkirk Wheel and the Kelpies and did lots of shopping.

Seonag talked to Dr. Joan about the two scans. Although she did look a bit confused at first, the doctor played it down, accepting the nurses' explanation. Seonag was convinced they had found something bad.

Chapter Five

It took weeks for the MRI result to come through. As time passed Iona tried to reassure her mother that had they found anything serious they would have been quicker, that no news is good news. Seonag was not convinced.

It was mid afternoon when Dr. Joan rang asking to speak to Matt. He had just come in from helping in the cafe and felt exhausted. Although he could be more active on the Risperdol it left him feeling permanently tired and sluggish. She told him that the MRI results were back. She did not want to talk about them over the phone, but could he come in to the surgery and see her that evening, she would see him after her last patient.

Matt retold the conversation to his hovering mother. "Can I come in with you?" She asked.
"As if I could keep you out," he quipped.
She was glad to hear him joke. Any news at this point would be good news, because then they could plan a way forward.

Seonag thought that Dr. Joan looked tired as she finally called them into her little office.

"Thank you, for seeing us today", Seonag really appreciated the personal interest the doctor had taken in helping Matt and the family.

"Well, I will tell you what I know, but I don't have all the answers. Mr. Rogers wants to see you next week. Sit down, do."

As they took their seats Joan pulled up a report on her computer screen.

"You were partially right Seonag about them finding something when they did the MRI, but they were not fibbing to you. The thing was they were not sure of what they had found, so they decided to do another fuller scan to make sure they had all the angles covered." She turned to Matt.

"You see, they were looking for a brain tumour as that can alsobe the cause of hallucinations. We didn't think you had one, because you don't have other symptoms of a tumour, but Mr. Rogers wanted to rule it out. You'll be glad to know that you don't have one." She paused and looked at her on screen notes.
"What you do have though is a condition called a 'Chiari Malformation'."

Seonag and Matt looked at each other, each none the wiser.

"I will explain it as best I can," continued Joan. "The good news is that it is curable. But the bad news is that you will have to have neurosurgery."

Matt didn't care about an operation, all he heard was the word curable and felt elated. There was an end in sight at last; he wasn't slowly going mad.

Dr. Joan went on to explain how there is a gap at the back of the skull where the brain tonsils meet the top of the spinal cord and basically it is how the brain is connected to the rest of your body. The MRI had shown that Matt had an obstruction in this gap, which meant that when he was excited, tired or had any stimulation that caused his brain to swell, the blockage would press into his brain. It had a similar effect to putting a break in a circuit board, sending everything haywire. The cure was an operation to cut the blockage away.

Matt was overjoyed and wanted to know how soon he could have the operation.

"Ah well," said Dr. Joan. "I can't say. There may be a problem finding a surgeon to do it. It has only been done thirteen times in Scotland before. Mr. Rogers will be able to tell you more about that. Also, your case is not straight forward."

"When can I see Mr. Rogers?" Matt could feel some of his old drive coming back.

"I spoke to him when your results came through today. He has seen them too. He is going to try and make space to see you next week. He will ring you directly."

Matt was walking on air as they left the surgery. "Are you ok about this operation? I suppose you have no choice." His mother asked when they were back in the car.

"Mum, I am not worried in the slightest," Matt beamed. "After the last few months it will be a breeze and I am sure they will have some mega painkillers." He laughed.

Mr. Rogers was as good as his word and offered Matt an appointment the following Wednesday. Iona could not go because of work commitments, so mother and son drove together to Inverness. Seonag had to put up with her son teasing her about being a nervous driver on the mainland, but she didn't mind. At last he was laughing again.

Mr. Rogers had grown quite fond of Matt and his family over the months. He admired his determination to get better and the obvious strength he took from his family support. He hadn't thought they would cope, but was pleased that they were doing so.

He didn't like being the one to burst Matt and Seonag's bubble, but he had to make sure they understood the risks. When he broached the fact that it wasn't quite as black and white as they had thought Matt tried to brush it off.

"I know operations have risks and that my condition is complicated," argued Matt. "I don't see what the problem is."

Rogers had to be blunt, which was hard for such a usually mild mannered man.

"Look, the risk isn't just that the anaesthetic will make you sick; it's sixty to forty that you will die. Also you have two conditions which are not fully understood and there are no guarantees that it will work even if you do survive it."

Seonag had paled slightly, but Matt was undeterred. "So it's a shot then?"

Rogers couldn't help but smile. "Look, the way I see it is that some people have PTSD and get treated and others are managing to live with Chiari malformations. However, there is anecdotal evidence that if you have both, the conditions exacerbate each other with devastating effects, which you know about. Yes this is a shot, but all I'm saying is I can't promise how good a shot it is."

"That's ok," replied Matt, "long shots are my speciality."

In another case Rogers might have advised against it but if anyone could pull through, he was sure Matt could.

Finding a surgeon was not easy either. A specialist in Glasgow agreed to take the referral, but for his own reasons wanted to monitor Matt himself for at least six months before agreeing to operate. Matt couldn't wait that long.

It was about a month later, on a Tuesday afternoon that they got a call from the Edinburgh Royal Infirmary. A surgeon called Linda Metters casually left a message for Matt to give her a call. After a brief chat, when Matt called her back, she invited that he should come to Edinburgh for a week long assessment and she would recommend a course of action after that. Matt was still slightly frustrated that she was still talking about assessing rather than doing but a week was better than a year. When she admitted that she had not actually done the operation before, just a similar one, Matt decided she was his kind of surgeon. "When can I expect an appointment?" he asked. He was expecting to be told that he would be written to in due course. "Can you be here by Thursday?" she replied.

Game on, thought Matt.

The Royal infirmary was an imposing grey stone construction, that exuded Edinburgh' historical medical roots. The Victorian exterior hid a maze of magnolia painted corridors, decorated with notice boards and avantgarde art work. You were guided to your ward or department by following the appropriately coloured line along the edge of the corridor. Matt had wondered how many people ended up in casualty from not looking where they were going.

The week's worth of tests turned out only to take three days. Later on Matt had little recollection of these days, he was so strongly medicated by that point. He did recall endless MRI scans taking pictures of his head from every angle. He had electrodes glued to his skull for other tests and had to sit through lots of cognitive assessments. He found it fun at first, but soon got bored, which allowed Figgy to run havoc around inside his head. The big strong marine hated the pale flaccid figure hugging his knees and rocking on the bed.

Seonag and her daughters stayed with Matt for the duration, taking turns to support him and help fend off Figgy.

They didn't actually meet Linda Metters until after the tests were complete. Seonag couldn't help but think that she was just a slip of a girl; she looked weighed down by the big bulky file she was carrying. She looked relieved as she plonked the file down on the table at the foot of his bed and offered her hand to Matt.

"Hello, I'm Linda. I take it you are Matt, Is it ok if I call you that? Boy have we gathered a lot of data on you."

Matt shook her hand, he didn't speak. He wanted her just to get on with what she had to say. This was too important for pleasantries. Miss Metters introduced herself to Seonag too, then pulled the curtain round the bed.

She sat on the end of the bed. "Shall I explain where we have got to?"

"Please," replied Matt.

"Well, unfortunately, our tests confirm the original diagnosis though the Chiari is worse than we thought, so I am definitely recommending neurosurgery as your best, well, probably only option. "

"When?" asked Matt

Miss Metters thought for a moment. "I will have to check, but probably next Wednesday."

Finally Matt smiled.

Seonag, wasn't quite so eager and wanted more details. "Mr Rogers mentioned some risks, what is your view on them?"

Miss Metters nodded to Seonag, but still talked directly to Matt. "Yes, it is pioneering neurosurgery. It is risky. This procedure has only been done about a dozen times in Scotland. I haven't actually done it before, but I have done some which were very similar."

Seonag had paled slightly, but Matt was still focussed.

"Will it work?"

"We think it is your best chance. I will shave the obstruction away from your brain tonsils, which will remove the pressure from your brain, which should allow you to function normally again. What we don't know is if there has been any permanent damage done already. However, if there is, it will make it easier to treat if it is not being exacerbated." She looked from mother to son and spoke a little more gently. "The other factor you should be aware of is that without the operation, the likelihood is that the condition will kill you within two years."

"I don't think I could live like this for another two years anyway," was Matt's sombre reply. "But hey, mum, shall we have a Ceilidh in two years then?"

" Absolutely," his mum squeezed his hand. Her heart was full of emotion. She was terrified for her son, but at the same time so proud of his bravery and fortitude. He squeezed her hand back.

"It's OK mum, this is good. I'm going to be better next week."

Miss Metters cautioned that recovery would be gradual. Matt would firstly have to recover from the operation, then they would slowly decrease the anti psychotic medication and only then they would be able to judge the extent of his recovery. Matt wasn't listening but Seonag devoured every word.

Miss Metters interrupted their thoughts. "The only thing we need to decide is what you want to do now. You can stay here if you want, but frankly we can do no more for you until the operation, so you are free to go, just come back by next Tuesday evening ready for the operation on Wednesday. Is that OK?"

Matt thought for a moment, then looked at his mother. "I think I'd like to go home mum, maybe see the family and perhaps we could go to church together on Sunday."

Matt had never been particularly religious. Seonag didn't know if he was saying that just for her, or maybe he was contemplating his own mortality. She didn't mind either way. With tears in her eyes she nodded in agreement.

The journey home felt long and the weekend went too quickly. They got home on the Friday, and would have to start back on the return journey on the Monday morning. Matt slept a lot, but on Sunday morning the whole family got themselves ready and went to Mass. Cousins, uncles, aunts and neighbours joined them. Special prayers were said for Matt and he was given the "sacrament of the sick." A few people gave him cards and people shook his hand. He laughed and joked about having to get a haircut and what he would be doing afterwards. Seonag sat quietly in the pew watching as he talked to people. "It's up to you now God," She prayed. "This is my son Lord, please look after him." In an odd sort of way, she felt at peace.

They got back home and put the kettle on. The plan was to have a bite to eat then start to pack for what could be an extended stay in Edinburgh. They were talking through the arrangements that had been made to look after things while they were away and what still had to be done. There was a knock on the kitchen door and then it opened. Their friend Pat MacDonald stood in the doorway balancing a large plate of sandwiches with a big bag on her arm full of goodies. "I knew you wouldn't have time to do anything, so I've brought a few things over."

She was closely followed by Marie and Phil, "Phil's made one of his famous chocolate cakes, we thought you might like it."

They were followed by Seonag's cousin Sketch and his wife with a box of homemade sausage rolls and a bottle. Rhona followed shortly with another bottle. When it was mentioned that Matt couldn't drink on his medication she retorted, "Who said it's for you? You're ok with this; the rest of us are scared shitless and need a drink." Matt had to smile.

People called in all afternoon. There were jokes and laughter, tears and hugs. The packing didn't get done until much later but the family felt much stronger knowing that they were not facing their ordeal alone.

Chapter Six

Seonag, Kate and Iona were at Matt's bedside as he waited for the operation the following Wednesday morning. They had been told that it would be first thing so when nothing had happened by eleven o'clock they were all feeling nervous.

Typically, Matt was most concerned about the fact that he hadn't eaten since the night before and was hungry.

"Mum, we're going to have to complain. They never told us about the risk of starvation." His mother gave him a weak smile.

"So what do you want afterwards?" asked Kate. "Anything you like, I will go and get it for you."

Matt thought for a moment. "Ben and Jerry's cookie dough ice cream." He smiled.

"Wouldn't you prefer the fish food?" asked Iona.

"Nope, cookie dough is the best."

The three of them began to debate the merits of different ice cream flavours. Seonag didn't join in, but was comforted by how her children supported each other.

When they finally took Matt down to theatre, her daughters tried to persuade Seonag to wander round the shops or see the sights in Edinburgh. She was having none of it however, she was adamant that she would wait by his bed.

"But mum, they said it's going to be about six hours, you can't sit here all that time." Iona tried to reason with her.

"I have to be where they can contact me," she argued.

It was no good, the best the girls could do was get her to go over the road to a coffee shop where she picked at a panini for half an hour before returning to the ward.

It was evening time before they were ushered in to the small high dependency ward. It was very quiet, apart from the constant bleeping of the various machines. Matt was barely conscious and looked frail and vulnerable. He was wearing an oxygen mask and his body was laced with tubes and wires. He moved involuntarily when he heard his mum's voice and moaned in pain. The nurses assured the family that all had gone well but that they were keeping him sedated overnight for pain management. They each gave him a kiss, before they left. "Love you," he murmured in his sleep.

Seonag didn't sleep that night and was up early, despite the fact that hospital visiting hours didn't start until two pm. She felt better after she rang the ward and was told that Matt was awake and had eaten breakfast, so she agreed to join her daughters on a stroll around the city.

"We have to get ice cream for Matt," reminded Iona.

"I thought you got that yesterday?" her mother asked.

"We did, but we ate it overnight," laughed Kate.
Seonag shook her head, which made both young women laugh even more.

"Oh c'mon mum, it wouldn't have kept and we had to do something." As Kate took her arm, Seonag realised that her daughters probably hadn't slept either.

It was a balmy September morning as they wandered round the old city. There was a lot going on; buskers, artists and street performers on every street, but none of them were really interested. At one o'clock, laden with fruit and ice cream they happily agreed to head back to the hospital.

Much to Seonag's relief, Matt was awake and smiling when they went in. Kate had to feed him the ice cream as he was not allowed to sit up due to the change in pressure in his head. Over the next few days they raised him gradually and by the end of the week he was sitting in the chair next to his bed. The staff and Miss Metters were very pleased with the speed of his recovery and he threw himself into physiotherapy, so it was not long before he was back on his feet. Figgy had gone and he was no longer passing out, but people were treating him as if he was still ill. He had no time for the medics telling him not to be too hard on himself. Working hard to achieve what he wanted was the only way he knew. He needed to make them understand that he had to get on with life and he didn't want to hear the warnings about possible relapses.

After two weeks it was agreed that he could finally be discharged, but with the stern warning from Miss Metters that he had to take things easy. She gave him what he considered an interminable list of things that he could not do, including no exercise for a month apart from the necessary physio.

Everyone was ecstatic about his return to Uist; his friends and family assuming that he felt the same way. He did, up to a point, but there were other things on his mind. He was impatient about the fact that the doctors were decreasing the antipsychotic drugs very slowly. He wanted to simply stop taking them, but had been warned that if he did he could have severe side effects. As he got better he became more self aware. Another effect of the drugs and the lack of exercise was that he had put on several stone in weight. He hated this, especially as plans for Iona's wedding were taking shape and he was to be giving his sister away. He didn't want to be recorded for posterity looking a slob. The way he looked and his lack of fitness were really bugging him.

The Navy had continued to support him and paid his salary for the duration and his commanding officer had rung every other week to check on his progress. He too seemed pleased with Matt's recovery but was politely evasive when Matt asked about a timescale for returning to work. This worried Matt too.

Physically Matt felt better than he had done in months, he just needed to get back to his old self. He knew that if he could take back control of at least one part of his life he would feel happier. He was counting the days to the end of his exercise embargo. He would work hard, get back into shape then he could go back to work. He had a plan.

December the seventeenth 2011 was the day Matt called "liberation day". That was the date it was officially agreed that he could start exercising again. The head of acute diseases, whom he travelled up to Stornoway to see on a weekly basis, insisted on adding the word "gentle" before "exercise" and Matt understood that. He knew that he wouldn't be lifting weights or kick boxing, but it would be a start; his start.

The trips to Stornoway had become annoying. It required an early start to get there and became increasingly difficult due to the limited winter travel timetables, shorter days and deteriorating weather. Once he arrived there followed a lot of sitting around just to wait for his hour long clinical assessment reviews. They were important though, as it was here that his withdrawal from the antipsychotic Risperadol was managed. They were quite intense sessions, where he repeatedly assured them that he hadn't heard Figgy lately and the scared little boy, whom he had come to realise was his mind's projection of his own feelings of vulnerability, had gone. He argued with the assessors that, even with the blockage at the back of his brain, his own will power and ability to distract himself had kept the hallucinations under control as much as the drugs had done. While they agreed with him to an extent, they still were cautious and unwilling to commit to a specific timetable for reducing the medication. This lack of a plan really infuriated Matt, but what made it worse was that he had to pretend to be calm and content as he did not want them to think he was ill again.

As it had been agreed by the hospital that he could start gentle exercises on December 17th and to help him do so, it would be a good point in his treatment to reduce the dosage by a third. The negative side effects of lethargy would be reduced which would help him exercise and the positive impact of endorphins would help him through any potential withdrawal problems.

The seventeenth was the Saturday before Christmas. The previous Christmas had been the family's first without his dad. It had been horrible, but what made it worse was that Matt had only made it back for a few days before flying out again. It was his work, he had no choice, but he felt bad about abandoning his mother in her grief. He had ended up talking about all this with his CPN and at the clinic. He was determined that this year would be better.

Matt had everything planned. He had arranged with Stuart, an old school friend, that they would go cycling around Eriskay. He had been working on his bike, so everything was ready. After that he had planned a regime of cycling and swimming to take him into the New Year after which he would start running. People wondered why he was specifically waiting so long before he started running as he had run competitively when he was younger. He didn't mention that he had tried to do so surreptitiously and had been so appalled by his inability and lack of fitness he knew that he couldn't start there, his self respect wouldn't let him.

Stuart had to come and collect him, as Matt would have to wait for a year from surgery before he could reapply for his driving licence which was another source of frustration. That morning however nothing bothered him. It was a bright clear day. By ten in the morning, the sky was a sparkling clear blue and the air had an invigorating winter crispness. It was a rare day for December in the Uists as there was very little wind but this made it ideal for cycling.

Matt had cooked himself his favourite breakfast, black pudding, a tattie scone and fried egg in a big roll. He didn't worry about the calories that morning because he was about to burn them off.

Stuart parked up at the Eriskay shop car park. From there they would be able to cycle around the island. It wasn't far in distance; the whole island was only one and a half by two and a half miles wide, but some of the single track road was very steep and it was challenging at the best of times.

"Listen matha," Stuart was putting on his cycling helmet. "I don't know about you, but I'm getting off at the steep bits. Don't want to break ourselves on our first trip out."

Matt laughed. "We'll see. The problem is, I am so unfit, I might not be able to walk up them either."

"Let's head for the old harbour and then round to Charlie's beach and we'll see how we feel then."

"C'mon then," Matt agreed, pulling out into the road. "No time like the present."

Matt was enjoying himself, although his legs ached and he was more breathless than he expected, he was really pleased to make it round past the old harbour toward the ferry slipway where the boat to Barra docked. Stopping to catch their breath, Matt was already thinking about the route back. The road up to the shop was very steep in places and he hadn't been entirely joking about his ability to push his bike up it.

"Instead of taking the main road back, why don't we cut off at the beach and take the track along the top that will bring us out at the Polly."

"Aye you just want to go to the pub Macaulay," Stuart teased, but agreed to cut across country to the Politician pub.

They set off again. Matt had always preferred off road cycling. This wasn't exactly challenging terrain but he could sprint and build up a little more speed without having to worry about traffic and it was a challenge to negotiate the different surfaces of sand, grass, rock and rabbit holes. The latter unfortunately was what Matt didn't see. The first thing he realised was that the bike was no longer moving but he was. As the front wheel jammed in a burrow, he went flying over the handle bars. Even after everything that had happened over the last year his training still kicked in. He was curled into a ball shape almost before he hit the ground and managed to roll so avoiding any broken limbs.

Stuart was immediately by his side. Matt sat himself up. "Take it easy matha, no rush to get up."

"I feel so stupid: schoolboy mistake and look at my bike." Matt pointed at his front wheel which wasn't the same shape that it had been five minutes earlier.

"Could easily have been me if I had been going first. These things happen," consoled Stuart.

"Aye, no real harm done I guess. We don't need to make a fuss of it when we get back eh?"

Stuart laughed at his friend. "How many war zones have you been in and you're still afraid to tell your mam you broke your bike. How you are going to hide that wheel?"

"Aye! It will go straight in the shed and hopefully she won't see it."

They chatted as they walked across the Machair towards the pub. Although nothing was broken, Matt did feel a bit achy and stiff after his tumble. By the time they got to the pub he had noticeably slowed down and looked very white.

Matt didn't argue when Stuart suggested that he wait with the bikes in the pub car park while Stuart went and got the car. Matt sat down at a wooden picnic table. His head and neck began to feel very heavy and a wave of dizziness and nausea surged through his body. Oh God don't let me pass out, he thought. He didn't but instead his head began throbbing so hard he felt he needed to hold onto his skull to keep it together.

Stuart wanted to drive him to the hospital, but Matt insisted that it was just a headache and he would sleep it off. "I didn't bang my head, probably just rattled it a bit," he tried to reassure his friend. They had only just driven back over the causeway, as far as West Kilbride on the very southern tip of South Uist, when Matt asked Stuart to stop the car. He was sick at the side of the road, not just once, but several times. After a few minutes, Matt thought he had finished, wiped his mouth and got back into the car. He felt awful, as bad as he had felt just after the operation but without the pain killers. They didn't get very far before they had to stop again on the main road. By the time they had stopped for a fourth time Stuart had made up his mind. He rummaged in his boot and found a couple of plastic carrier bags. He put one inside the other. He'd noticed that Matt had lost most of his breakfast and was just vomiting bile now, but the retching looked agonising. As Matt got back into the car, he handed him the bags and told him what was going to happen.

"I'm not stopping again; you're getting worse each time. If you feel sick, puke up in that, I'm driving straight to the hospital."

Matt felt too weak to argue. He started to explain to Stuart another of the warnings he had been given that he might have overlooked.

"I know what this is. When they did the op, it was close to what I think they called the sick centre, it's at the back of the head." He paused to try and stop himself retching again. "The thing is, once this, whatever it is, is disturbed, if you throw up you can't stop." Matt was sick into the bag.

"Well hopefully they'll give you a jag or something at the hospital then."

Matt agreed; he also hoped they would give him something for the pain in his head.

The Uist and Barra Hospital did not have an A&E department as such. Nurses treated minor injuries in the outpatients department and for anything more serious, the duty doctor was called in.

Stuart screeched to a stop outside the main entrance, he didn't bother with the car park. He helped Matt out of the car and supported him into the foyer. As they walked along the corridor to Out Patients Matt was still trying to be sick into his bag.

"Hello, help anyone!" Stuart called out now bearing most of his friend's weight. A nurse popped her head round the corner. On seeing the pair of them she immediately fetched a wheel chair and they took Matt into a side room. While she assisted Matt, the staff nurse called the duty doctor and hoping that he or she wouldn't be too far away, Stuart rang Seonag.

The duty doctor, Andrew Marks, lived on Benbecula, so arrived quickly. He immediately gave Matt the anti sickness injection and while it was taking effect started asking questions about the headache. The medical practice had a system alert covering their seriously ill patients, so although he hadn't treated him personally, he was aware of Matt's surgery and knew generally about his condition.

Matt was trying to sit up, rather than lie down on the bed. He was sweating with the pain and now looked very grey.

"I didn't bang my head," he insisted. "It's to do with the sickness. It's worse when I'm trying to be sick or lying down. I'm better sitting up, well, a bit anyway."

Dr. Marks decided to ring Edinburgh Infirmary for advice. Seonag and Iona arrived at Matt's bedside just as he came back with news of his conversation. He didn't beat about the bush.

"OK, So I spoke with Miss Metter's registrar. They want to admit you immediately, I have arranged for the air ambulance to transport you; it should be here within the hour."
"Why, what for?" Matt demanded; he didn't want to go back. "I only fell off my bike, I just want some pain killers."

"They don't want to take that risk and are preparing surgery for an emergency lumbar puncture."

Doctor Marks wasn't about to debate any further, I'm going to give you something for the pain and to prepare you for the journey; it will probably send you to sleep."

Matt looked as if he was going to cry. The doctor softened his tone, "I'm sorry, but we have no option. Get it done today and all being well you will probably be home for Christmas."

Matt sat back against the cushions, he didn't object any further. Tears welled up in the corners of his eyes as he listened to Stuart trying to explain to his mother what happened. "Well, that's me busted," he thought as he faded into unconsciousness.

Both Iona and Seonag were crying as they watched Matt being wheeled into the ambulance to be driven the short distance to the airport. They followed the ambulance as far as they could, then standing pressed up against the security fence watched the gurney being loaded onto a small helicopter. As it took off Seonag and Iona couldn't help themselves and sobbed into each other's arms. Stuart had come with them and he too was overwhelmed. It was crazy, his heart ached for his friend, after all he had been through, wanting just to ride your bike was surely not too much to ask.

Chapter Seven

Matt was awake, but he didn't want to open his eyes. He was trying to piece together where he was and what had happened. He was fairly sure he was in hospital by the feel of the bed. He felt very weary and his head hurt but he was sure that it did not hurt as much as it had done before. Why did it hurt? He asked himself, he'd had the operation ages ago, he had been discharged and... Then it came to him, he'd been on his bike. "Oh shit," he muttered.

"Is that a sign of life brother dear?"

He smiled, at the sound of Kate's voice. "Am I in trouble?"

"Big trouble boy, but I am sure you will be forgiven, how are you feeling?"

"I'm not sure, better I think. What day is it? Did they do whatever they were going to do?"

"It's Sunday afternoon. They did the lumbar puncture yesterday evening. They say it went ok, seemingly they drained off a lot of whatever gunk you had on your brain and say you should feel better for it. That is all they would tell me and said they'd be in to speak with you later."

"Gunk? Was that the medical term?"

"Absolutely."

Matt eased himself up, he was relieved to find the movement didn't cause shooting pains in his head and he wasn't feeling sick. In fact, he actually felt a little peckish.

The doctors made their rounds around teatime. They explained that there had been a build up of fluid in his brain which had been causing pressure and that they had drained this away. The procedure had been a success and as long as he remained stable, they would look to discharge him on Monday to go home and rest for Christmas. Matt asked them why it had happened; had it occurred when he fell off the bike? The doctor suspected that the accident probably didn't help, but that this was a post operation complication which could happen to anyone who had had neurosurgery. Matt nearly asked him to put that in writing because he suspected he would never be able to convince his mother.

Kate had planned to travel home for Christmas herself on the Tuesday, so it was agreed that they would travel back together. Matt wasn't exactly looking forward to going home. He didn't want to be wrapped in cotton wool again, Christmas or not.

It was a subdued Christmas in the Macaulay household that year. The younger generation missed their dad and Seonag her husband. They were all weary, pulled down by grief, worry and uncertainty. They had got through it but the latest emergency with Matt had really shaken all of them. Matt didn't argue, he rested and let his mother fuss over him; he could put up with it for a short while at least. Kate and Matt returned home just in time, as the weather closed in for the festive season. It wasn't pretty festive snow, but dark, bleak, unrelenting rain and wind that sapped their spirits further. The family, however, were not the kind of people to mope. As the new year approached, and the sky cleared they gained a collective second wind and a determination to make the coming year a better one.

Kate had to go back to the mainland after the holidays and wanted to get out and enjoy the hills before she left. She was a naturally active person, who couldn't stand being cooped up for too long. Iona had gone to spend a few days with her fiancé's family, so it was only the three of them in the house.

"Does anyone fancy going up Ben Mhor? Matt?" she asked one morning at breakfast.

Matt thought for a moment. "D'you know, I'd love to."

Seonag said nothing, but looked a little worried. Kate, however, had thought things through.

"You still have the all clear for gentle exercise don't you? It's not a hard walk and the forecast is good. We may not get much further than the foothills, but you have to start somewhere and I need to stretch my legs or I am going to go barmy."

"You could take the dog too," suggested Seonag, indicating that she grudgingly approved.

Once the decision was made it didn't take them long to wrap up in their fleeces and waterproofs, grab a few snacks and head out. They needed to be quick as there wasn't much daylight at the turn of the year. They walked for about four hours and talked from time to time of their plans for the coming year but mostly they walked in companionable silence, just soaking up the views and enjoying the freedom of the wild terrain. When they stopped for a slurp of juice and their snack bar it was obvious that Matt was tired. Kate didn't comment. She suggested they should walk for another half an hour then turn back to ensure they had plenty of daylight to come back down. Matt agreed. As they made their descent he was slower. His thigh muscles and lower back ached but he didn't complain; he loved every minute of it. By the time they got back to the car though, he was exhausted.

Kate drove a short way and pulled over into a passing place and stopped the car. She turned and put her hand on his arm. "Now listen, brother of mine, promise me that you are going to do that, or something like it every day now. Nothing too risky, but push yourself a little further each time. Next time I see you will be at Iona's wedding in the summer. I love you matha, and look forward to seeing the change in you then." She leaned over and gave him a hug. Matt hugged her back; she was right and he knew he was going to do it.

Matt didn't quite make it every day, but he did most. By the end of January the days began to get longer again and he was out and about as much as he could. He saw it as his job to get himself fit and well and back to work. During his training and long walks he did a lot of thinking. His plan was to support his mum and sister with the arrangements for the wedding, then once declared fit and medication free, concentrate on getting his own career back on track. He continued to help his friends by working in the cafe and even went out with Stuart Steele on his boat. He joined the training sessions with the local football team, the Saints. He enjoyed the team spirit, although he didn't quite make the first team. The trips to Stornoway became monthly instead of weekly and his medication dosage decreased. By Iona's wedding day on the fourth of June he had lost two stone in weight and was on a minimal "holding dose" of the Risperadol, prior to stopping it completely.

The weather was glorious on June the fourth. The bride was beautiful and the little church at Bornish packed with family and friends. He knew that his mother was going to find the day hard without her husband at her side which made him determined to be there for her. He was on form, joking that he was too young really to be the father of the bride, but was just practising for years to come and speaking confidently about returning to the navy by the end of the year. They danced to the early hours, and continued the following day with the house wedding; a local custom for closer friends and family. There were tears and laughter; the MacAulay family finally had a reason to celebrate.

The celebrations continued into July and August when Matt was finally declared medication free and discharged from medical care. Dr. Simpson told him that a letter would be sent to his commanding officer. Matt decided the right thing to do was tell him in person and perhaps discuss what happened next. Matt was a little disappointed at the call as he only got to speak with the adjutant who, while congratulating him on his recovery, was somewhat formal in his response. He told Matt that after they received the formal notification from his doctor they would write to him then. Matt didn't know the man and decided to ring round a few people that he did know to see if he could arrange an early appointment. He knew he couldn't just turn up on spec but he wanted to get the ball rolling.

He didn't have to wait too long; very soon a letter arrived inviting him to attend a meeting in a month's time in Plymouth. He wished it was sooner but was still pleased. Finally things would get back to normal. Despite his fitness regime, he could only just get into his old uniform; he had more work to do, so maybe the month long wait was a good thing.

It was arranged for Matt to fly from Benbecula to Glasgow, then south to Exeter Airport, where he would be picked up. He was to stay on base overnight, then meet a Lieutenant Commander Thornton the following morning. Matt thought it was odd that Thornton was described as his Contact Officer.

Matt was shown to a room in the Officers' Mess, he found it strange that everything looked exactly the same. It was as if time had stood still, when so much had changed in his own world. He was hanging up his uniform ready for the next morning when his phone rang. He sighed as he picked it up. Still checking up on me he thought. He was wrong, well at least partially. Seonag did ask if he had any problems flying and to make sure that he didn't have a headache, but was more excited to let him know that his sister Iona was pregnant. She had told her mother the news shortly after Matt had left. The baby was due the following Easter. Matt was really pleased and viewed it as a good omen. When he rang his sister to congratulate her he was in a buoyant mood, ready for his interview the next morning.

It felt good wearing his uniform again. Matt brushed himself down before his interview; he didn't know Thornton and wanted to make sure he made the right impression. It did cross his mind that had he been off for 18 months with cancer or a physical injury it would not be such an issue but when it was all about your head it changed things. He was just going to have to prove them wrong.

Thornton was a polite full faced man, with a dark beard that was failing to hide his double chin. His eyes were small and slightly overactive when he looked Matt up and down as he entered the room. He congratulated Matt on his recovery and expressed pleasure at seeing him so well. Matt smiled but wondered why as they had not met before. After inviting Matt to take a seat, Thornton shuffled his papers and cleared his throat and got on with what he had to say.

"The thing is of course Captain, we have received the NHS assessment of you, but we, ehm, expect a bit more of our marines than the NHS do out of an ordinary chap, do you see what I mean?"

"Yes sir." Matt had expected some sort of re-assessment.

"Having discussed your file with our senior medical people, they tell me that they need you to undertake medical, fitness and stress tests before they can make a recommendation. I can arrange for these to take place in our training centre in Inverness if that is more suitable for you."

I'm back with the recruits, Matt thought, but simply replied with a professional "Yes sir, Thank you sir."

"Excellent! Unless you have any questions Macaulay? That is about us. Thank you for coming down."

Matt was a bit annoyed about having to make a four day round trip for a twenty minute discussion but he was not overly surprised, he knew that the bureaucratic cogs had to turn, it was just as well that his operational managers had not been like that.

"I do have a question sir. Have you got a timescale for these tests?"

"Yes, good question, I should have mentioned it. We want to get things wrapped up by the end of the year, so basically as soon as my Sergeant can arrange them. You have had a notable if short career to date. The Navy and indeed country have been in your debt on a number of occasions so I understand. We will not keep you waiting unnecessarily for a decision."

Matt couldn't argue with what had been said, but he didn't like the inference. "I intend to stay in the Navy sir."

"I know, I know, but you will have to convince the quacks."

Thornton sounded impatient, he looked at his watch; he obviously had somewhere else to be and wanted to conclude the conversation. Matt decided not to prolong his agony. He understood that it wouldn't be Thornton's decision anyway. He thanked him politely and arranged his lift back to the airport. He didn't want to hang around on base, it didn't feel quite like it used to.

Thornton was as good as his word. Letters came through for a medical examination and fitness test within a couple of weeks of Matt's return home. He had been training hard and was pleased to have a date to be focussed on. As he was getting stronger, his sister was having difficulties as her pregnancy was proving not to be straightforward. She was very sick in the early stages and the baby was deemed to be on the small side. Matt tried to suggest that it might be because she didn't eat meat, but she didn't appreciate his attempt at humour and reminded him that falling off bikes straight after neurosurgery wasn't too clever either.

Matt did have a nagging worry in the back of his mind that the navy might consider him too much of a risk to take him back. But everyone was so pleased with his recovery and he felt bad trying to explain that things might not be as rosy for him as they seemed. He was also conscious of the concern over Iona's health and felt he had been enough of a burden already. Matt did the only thing he could do and that was to work hard: he would simply give them no choice by proving their fears unfounded.

His training paid off, as after his trip, the medical officer reported that he was pleased and surprised to report that Captain Macaulay had passed both medical and fitness tests with flying colours. Matt was really pleased with himself. Halfway there, he thought.

He was then invited to a stress test and psychological assessment. Matt knew this was going to be harder. It had taken him long enough to be able to talk to the Community Nurse about how he felt, never mind a man in uniform with a clip board. He did understand and respect his employers' need to do so. Whilst it was difficult, he viewed the fact that he was able, at least briefly, to describe the last eighteen months and how he dealt with Figgy, proved to himself that he was even stronger now than before his illness.

In October Matt was overjoyed to receive a copy of his psychological assessment, stating that he had no mental health issues.

"Look at this", he laughed as he read the letter out to his mother. "That's two doctors reckon I'm sane. They can't both be mistaken." He was expecting it to be just a matter of time before he was given a starting date. "I realise that there's going to be some tedious re-training, but I can get through that," he would explain when asked. As much as he loved his home and was grateful for the support he had been given, he needed his life and his sense of purpose back.

To pass his time Matt was helping out on a charity project to restore old buildings on the island. It kept him fit and got him out and about. As the autumn was drawing in though and the days were getting colder, it was a bit less attractive than it had been in the summer time.

He came home one evening and headed straight over to the Aga in the kitchen. His intention was to sit on it for as long as he could, in order to get some heat back into his body. His mother came in and they exchanged the news of the day. Seonag had been to an appointment with Iona, and was concerned about the fact that the midwife wanted to undertake more tests.

"Her husband's away and she is running round like a blue arsed fly for Social Services, who do not appreciate her. That poor girl has no peace; that's why her blood pressure is up. You don't need fancy tests to diagnose that." Seonag was clearly annoyed and worried for her daughter. Matt put the kettle on for tea; it was the only cure when his mum was in this frame of mind.

"She was talking of stopping early herself the other day."

"Yes, as long as she rests when she does. You know what she's like." Seonag took her tea as Matt shrugged his shoulders in half hearted agreement.

"She won't cope with sitting around, mum."

Seonag shook her head in mock frustration. "How did I get such stubborn children?"

"I blame the parents," Matt teased.

Sipping her tea, Seonag suddenly remembered. "Oh, there's a letter for you. I put it on the side."

Matt recognised the familiar postmark on the envelope on the dresser. He felt a rush of excitement as he picked it up. Could this be it, could the nightmare finally be over?

Chapter Eight

The letter however was not quite what Matt had expected. He was really pleased to see that it was signed by Commander Goddard, his commanding officer rather than the cold fish Thornton. It didn't however make reference to any of his recent tests or interviews; it simply invited Matt to join the Commander for a meeting when he came up to visit 45 Commando in Arbroath in a couple of weeks. There was a phone number to call. Matt felt uneasy.

"He surely can't mean you to go to Arbroath?" his mother was as confused as Matt. "Does he know where we live?"

"Yes, I have spoken to him about the islands before. He always said that he would like to come and visit. Not this time I guess. I will give him a ring in the morning." Matt had already tried the phone number given. It was after six in the evening and the phone had gone to voicemail. He didn't leave a message.

It was the Commander's secretary that Matt spoke to the next morning. He explained that Commander Goddard would be flying into Glasgow airport at the end of the week for a series of meetings around Scotland and wanted to see Matt while he was there. Matt knew that while the secretary made it sound like a polite request, he really had no option but to attend.

The time and place in Glasgow were agreed, they would meet at Kentigern house, on Friday lunchtime, which gave Matt time to fly in and home again on the same day if he so wished. Matt wasn't looking forward to the meeting. One moment he would be pleased because it was what he had been waiting for; he had passed all their tests, so it should be fine. On the other hand, he had a deep sense of foreboding. What would he do if his worst fears were realised?

His family were more worried about him than they had been in a long time. He was very subdued before the meeting and had refused Kate's offer to meet up for a drink afterwards. That was not like him.

From the airport he took the bus into the city centre. It was only a short walk to the Ministry of Defence office block. From the outside it matched the Georgian facade of metropolitan Glasgow. Inside, the magnolia paint and yellowing gloss could have been any military HQ in the world. He arrived early.

After having his identity and invitation confirmed, he was given a pass and shown into a small waiting room where he was offered tea. He declined. I've been here before he thought.

The Commander greeted him warmly and his joy to see Matt in good health seemed genuine. He recapped some of Matt's exploits and congratulated him on his career. As he spoke, he was confirming Matt's worse fears. This was beginning to sound like his epitaph.

"You had us worried a couple of times," sighed the Commander. "Especially over the last couple of years. Took a strong man to get through that."

Here we go, thought Matt, he's cutting to it now.

"Thank you sir, all I want is to plan for the future now sir and get back to work."

The commander took a deep breath, choosing his next words carefully. "I am really sorry to have to tell you, that while I am really confident that you will be exemplary in whatever you choose to do, it cannot be in the military."

Although Matt was half expecting something like that, it still hit him in the chest. For a moment he was stunned, lost for words. Suddenly the nonsense and injustice of it hit him as if from a left jab followed by a right hook. "But why, sir? I passed all of the medical and fitness evaluations and my record, as you just said, proves what I can do..."

"I know, I know," the commander interrupted him. "It is nothing to do with any of that. It's the simple fact you have had neurosurgery and your skull is no longer intact which disqualifies you from military service."

"But you re-post people with PTSD and injuries every day, I've seen it happen," Matt blurted.

"Not those who have had surgery like yours we don't."

Matt had to breathe deeply to remain calm, although half of him wondered if he should just let rip; this man whom he had always regarded as someone to look up to had just stabbed him in the back.

"Well if you knew that, why did you make me do all those assessments then? You knew straight after my op or even before it. Why didn't you say then?" His voice was beginning to break with strain.

"The medics didn't think you were well enough to be told that sort of news while you were recovering from your operation. As for the assessments, that was down to me I'm afraid. I wanted to buy some time to argue your case, your being demonstrably fit and well, I thought might strengthen my argument. But I failed. I'm so sorry."

Goddard did look truly sorry. Matt wasn't angry with him. He was angry with life, with fate, with everything. He tried to search for options that could be considered.

"Who do I need to contact to appeal? What about a job on base?"

"I've been through all that Macaulay. You know that we all have to be operationally ready and you now can never be, because of the surgery. I'm sorry." He handed Matt an envelope. "It is explained fully in here, but I felt that I owed you the courtesy to tell you myself."

"Matt wanted to swear but managed to stifle it to a "Humph."

Having broken the news, there was very little else the Commander could say. He stood up and patted Matt on the shoulder. "It has been an honour serving with you Captain. I am really sorry this can't end another way. I have to go as I have another meeting but you take your time if you need to before you leave. There are some papers to sign which we will send by post."

Matt stood up and shook his hand wearily. He couldn't speak and definitely didn't want to stay there. He picked up the envelope and left.

Seonag didn't like the fact that Matt wasn't answering his phone. He had told her that he wasn't sure whether he would be coming home that evening, so she wasn't altogether surprised when he wasn't on the afternoon flight. However, as it got later her anxieties increased. She rang Kate, who was working in Glasgow, to ask if she had heard from him. When the answer was no, Seonag started to cry. She was scared for him, she couldn't bear for anything to happen to him now after all he had been through.

Kate sighed, she was a journalist, so didn't work regular hours as such, but was just thinking about heading home. "OK Mum. Would you like me to go round a few pubs to see if I can find him?"

Seonag was relieved. "Would you? Thank you darling. I would really appreciate it."

Kate thought that her mother was probably over reacting, but knew she would wind herself up until she had heard more. "I'll try some of his usual haunts and tell him to give you a ring. But I'm not interrupting if he is with some short skirted lassie." Kate's attempt at humour didn't work, so she promised her mother that either she or Matt would call her later to let her know what had happened.

It was a cold, dreich night. The drizzle hung in the air and soaked into every miniscule gap in her clothing, finding its way through to the bone marrow. Kate had her hood up and hands stuffed deep into her pockets as she trudged the streets looking for her brother. When he wasn't in the Park Bar or O'Neill's, she started to systematically make her way from pub to pub. Cold and wet, she was beginning to get fed up with her brother. She tried to call him, but she couldn't hear her phone in the pubs and when she rang, standing in wet doorways, he wasn't picking up. Kate didn't panic easily, so didn't imagine he was in danger, she just needed to get to him before he was.

About an hour later the Friday night crowd was beginning to build up. Kate pushed her way through the crowded Wetherspoons bar by Central Station. There were Hen parties and groups of blokes from works do's all celebrating or drowning their sorrows. She paused to gather her thoughts and work out where to go next.

"You by yourself handsome, gonna make space for a bit of company?" It was a large brassy blonde, who was addressing someone in a corner who was obscured by a pillar. Kate didn't hear the reply, but the blonde's friend, a short dark, spiky looking woman retorted, "Hey, there's no need tae be like that. You've got a whole table and this place is heavin'."

Curious, Kate leaned round the pillar and breathed a sigh of relief. She'd found him. Matt looked dishevelled and red eyed. In front of him was a half finished pint glass and several shot glasses and his phone lay on top of a tattered looking envelope. She didn't know how long he had been there, but they obviously weren't his first drinks of the night.

"Hey Matt," she called as she squeezed by the two girls. "He's with me, we'll be gone in a minute."

Matt looked up as she squeezed in beside him. "Hello sis," he slurred.

"What're you doing here? Is your phone not working?"

"I didnae want to talk to anyone." He sounded very dejected.

"You had a bad day then? I take it meeting the big man didn't go as you'd hoped."

"You could say that." He took another slurp from his glass. "D'you want a drink?"

"Na, I'd rather get out of here. I'm soaked to the skin looking for you."

"You didn't have to. I'm a big boy now, I can get pished if I like."

"Yeah, but not without telling someone where you are."

"Mam sent ye."

"Yep, c'mon we can have a drink at mine. I got a bottle of T bag at home you can demolish if it makes you feel better. I'm packed up for moving, but we can sit on boxes and drink it and you can tell me what happened."

Matt looked like he was about to argue, but he didn't have the energy. "Your sofa's not packed?"

"No, you can kip on that." Matt was oblivious to his belongings as she helped him to his feet. Kate picked up the phone and the envelope, presuming that it was his and guided him through the crowd out of the pub. As the cold air hit him, the alcohol took full effect and he buckled leaning against her. He started to heave. "Don't puke on me now matha. Hold it in while we get a taxi."

The first couple of cabs she tried to flag down drove on by, wary about the state Matt was in. Finally one stopped and agreed to take them out of town. He looked at Matt suspiciously. Kate assured the driver that she had cash and would pay if Matt was sick, although luckily it didn't come to that.

They didn't talk that night. Matt emptied most of the contents of his stomach into her toilet then crashed on her sofa leaving the bottle of Te Bheag whisky untouched. Kate was worried that he would keep on being sick, but the volume of alcohol he had consumed had the overriding effect of knocking him out. The next morning he had the hangover from hell.

Between cups of coffee and the pain killer Tramadol, Matt told the gist of what had happened at the meeting. "Och I am so sorry, Matt." She really felt for him. "But you can see where he is coming from, if it is more dangerous for you in a combat zone or whatever..."

"No, I can't!" he interrupted." If a bomb goes off everyone gets it. I can't believe they can't find me anything. You read the effing letter. They won't even have me in the TA. It's not on. I'm gonna write and complain. I was thinking of calling Angus Brendan last night."

Angus Brendan MacNeil, a Barra man, was their local member of parliament. "You didn't call him last night did you?" Kate asked cautiously.

"No, I couldn't get the phone to work," Matt muttered.

"Well let's be thankful for small mercies, it wouldn't have done your case any good."

Matt got himself together to take the evening flight home. Kate was relocating to house sit in Fort William for a friend, after which she would join the family for Christmas.

Matt was subdued when he got home. He had to endure his mother's remonstrations about not telling her where he was. "I could hardly tell her I was going out on the lash," he confided to Iona, but got no sympathy from his sister who had been worried too. The atmosphere was made worse by the fact that his family and friends all seemed to understand the navy's position. Whilst they agreed that they could have found something for him, they just didn't understand how utterly devastated he felt. Being back on active service had been his one happy thought that had kept him going through the darkest of times and now that had gone. Instead of understanding, the people around him seemed relieved. He was not some invalid to be written off, he needed a challenge. He needed a plan.

Chapter Nine

Seonag was determined not to have yet another glum Christmas and put all her efforts into emphasising the positives.

Matt, on the other hand, concentrated on ignoring Christmas. He worked hard at the renovation project. The navy had offered him a generous severance payment, so he wasn't worried about money but needed to fill his time and be active.

In the evenings he wrote letters to everyone he could think of challenging the decision, but while he got sympathetic replies, nobody would over-ride the medical judgement. As the festivities grew closer Matt's mood became darker. He found it hard to hear about anything related to the military without feeling angry. The final straw came when he heard a news flash on the radio when he was working; reporting that three marines had been killed in Helmand province. Matt did not know them personally but nonetheless felt overwhelmed with grief. He went outside and wept uncontrollably.

The family were fretting about how subdued and angry he was. Their concern added to his sense of frustration. This was not the same as last time; this time he knew why he was angry and with whom. He tried to explain that being sane doesn't mean he had to be happy all of the time, but he didn't think they got that either.

Christmas day was still better than the year before as at least this time the hospital references were about babies and not him. In the afternoon Seonag reminded them that their Aunt Liz was coming round to spend Boxing Day with them. Liz was a nurse, not just by profession, but also as a passion. "That's you two being analysed for the day then," Kate teased her siblings. "Hope you have your full medical notes filed properly and she'll want to inspect your scar too."

"If she tries to examine me I will throw up on her!" Iona retorted. "C'mon Kate, you need to share the load. Can't you think of some weird symptom to ask her about?" she begged.

Matt laughed at his sister's jokes, but knew that they weren't exaggerating that much. His aunt did like to inspect the back of his head and would look intently into his eyes when he spoke.

The evening was spent quietly drinking and watching television. Every now and then one of them would say something like "backward facing toes" or "inverted pubic hairs" and they would all laugh, which thoroughly confused and mystified Seonag, which only made them laugh even more.

The next morning Matt lay in bed, starring lazily out of the window. It was a clear day and the hills looked sharp. He had loved that view ever since he was a small boy. A smile crossed his face as he remembered last winter when Kate had dragged him up the hill and given him a talking to. He had felt like shit, but he had to keep up with her. He laughed at the memory. She had been right though, starting with small steps that day he had made himself better. He got up and opened the curtains wider. The distant rocks glinted invitingly in the sun. Perhaps I should do another Christmas run, he mused. It would get me out of the house and maybe, just maybe, I'll find inspiration again. "You never know unless you try," he sighed as he rummaged in his wardrobe for his hiking boots.

As he laced up his boots he wondered how he could tell them what he was going to do and why he needed time out but each time he ran through it in his head it sounded silly. "I just won't tell them till I get back," he decided.

He'd done lots of walks and training for those stupid fitness tests which turned out to be a complete waste of time. He pulled his laces harder as he was reminded of his anger and frustration. Last Christmas he had to drag himself up the mountain, just to prove to himself that he would be able to recover. Today he wanted to run it to... he thought further for a moment... to what? To be himself. To run off all that had been bugging him and his need to be what people thought he was. Maybe then, he might be able to find a way forward.

Unnoticed, he strode through the gate and took the track to the hills. Little did he know how this small act was about to change everything.

******

Don't miss Matt's further adventures in Hebridean Storm, the first volume of The Matt Macaulay Trilogy by Libby Patterson.

Printed in Great Britain
by Amazon